RIN

Jo loved Blair, had loved him for a long time—but he had chosen another girl and there was nothing she could do about it except try to hide the heartbreak. The abrasive presence of Marsh McConnell might be what she needed to shake her out of her despondency—except that it might possibly have a different effect on her . . .

RING OF FIRE

BY

MARGARET WAY

MILLS & BOON LIMITED
17–19 FOLEY STREET
LONDON W1A IDR

First published 1978
Philippine copyright 1978
This edition 1978

© Margaret Way 1978

ISBN 0 263 72599 5

Set in Linotype Times 10 on 10½ pt.

Made and printed in Great Britain by
Richard Clay (The Chaucer Press), Ltd., Bungay, Suffolk

Pammy

CHAPTER ONE

Jo thought the night would never end. Only the knowledge that people were watching kept her appalled, suppressed emotions from spilling over. It took an enormous effort of will, an auxiliary discipline she didn't
even know she possessed, but anything was better than
showing her true feelings. That would have been too
intolerable a humiliation. This should have been *her*
night, the beginning of a blissful existence. But all her
dreams, the visions she had nourished, had been brutally
snatched away from her. The future seemed no more
than a wasteland. Over the house she had loved all her
life and looked on as a second home hung a pall of
misery and rejection. Why didn't the ground simply open
and swallow her up? No one would really miss her. Now,
much too late, she had found out what manner of man
Blair was. The bitter truth was, she still loved him.
Nothing could change that. She had given him her heart
too long ago and she was stupidly, fiercely loyal, even
now. All she had to sustain her through this long, dreadful evening was a desperate kind of pride.

For days now, woman-like, she had made every manner of excuse for him. After all the things he had said, all
the promises, it didn't seem possible this was happening.
He *couldn't* be in love with somebody else, unless he was
an accomplished deceiver. He had violated her love and
her trust, yet every time their eyes met she was frightened by the raw wave of feeling that seemed to link them
so powerfully. There was sensuality in those wide-
spaced, slanted amber eyes and a kind of repressed
laughter, almost as if this big, beautiful, expensive engagement party was no more than a joke and he had

5

turned into someone she didn't even know.

The emptiness, the frozen numbness would come, but for now her shocked reaction was so damaging it was making her ill. Even more surprising were the whispers of 'beautiful' that followed her as she went through the motions of helping Aunt Elizabeth and pretending enjoyment when she really had no idea what she was doing at all. Did no one guess at the fiends of jealousy and betrayal that pursued her? Everywhere she had gone at this big, hectic party, she would have been astonished at the image of sparkling vivacity she was projecting, but the effort was using up all her nervous strength. She had a splitting headache and there was no way she could retire before it was all over. Aunt Elizabeth relied on her. Aunt Elizabeth, too, had once said she was proud to a fault. At least that much-discussed quality in her was coming to her aid. No one here tonight, relatives, friends, almost everyone in the district, could be entirely unaware of her feelings for Blair. It seemed to her now that she had loved him all her life and she had never been one to hide her affections.

Like a nymph, frozen in her secret misery, she stole out into the garden. It was a beautiful, soft night, overhung by a glittering net of stars, pervaded by the summer scent of gardenias. Such beauty, the profound and moving tenderness of night increased her grief. She couldn't resist it. Here on just such a romantic night Blair had taken her in his arms and kissed her into a breathless submission. If she thought of it in this tropical darkness she would start to cry. There were coloured lanterns and lamps in the trees and twenty or more tables set out at intervals on the velvety lawn, but now after supper nearly everyone had gone back inside or were dancing on the terrace. Jo turned her head and as an added torture saw Blair with Julie closely wrapped in his arms. They were moving dreamily to the music that spilled out of the house, Blair's handsome golden-

skinned face half hidden in Julie's soft primrose curls.
Her sweet, heart-shaped little face was so radiant, so
much the face of a woman in love, it was almost impossible to grudge her her place in Blair's arms.

'Blair!' Jo said in a whisper that didn't belong to her.
My love! My heart's desire! Dearest liar and cheat!
Her heart contracted and for a dreadful moment she
thought she was going to be sick. It was almost as if she
no longer had control. He had never seemed so desirable
to her, so handsome, so unattainable. She felt her face
give a nervous spasm of pain and she flung out her hand
in the age-old gesture of protest and despair. How could
he have lied to her? How could he have promised to
marry her and make all those plans when all along he
had decided in his mind to marry Julie. Only a scoundrel
could act with so little decency—a sadist. He was totally
different from everything she had believed. She had
given him qualities he had never possessed, but how did
one go about killing feeling? There was no opiate, no
drug she wouldn't have tried then.

Now nearing the end of a brilliant engagement party,
she was going to strike the only discordant note and
show all these watching, waiting, friends of a lifetime
they had been right after all. It wouldn't even cause a
sensation, but it would create an unpleasant situation
and bring pain to Aunt Elizabeth and Uncle Joss when
she owed them so much. One day the unbelievable,
would happen: she would recover—she wasn't the first
woman to suffer this blinding assault on her pride and
self-esteem. She gave a funny little cry. She couldn't
seem to help it. She knew she was swaying. If she could
only make it to one of the tables. The last thing she
wanted to do was make herself a talking point...

Out of nowhere a man materialised, a tall man moving like a shadow and graceful as a panther taking her in
formidably strong arms before she surely sank to the
ground. She started to protest, unbearably antisocial in

her misery but he ignored her completely.

'Are you all right?'

'I'm sorry!' Jo was shocked into apologising.

'Oh, for what?'

'I was a million miles away.'

'I should try to get over it!'

The tone was so odd she turned her head up to stare at him, only then becoming aware of his identity. 'Mr McConnell!'

'At least you remember my name, but you still haven't answered my question.'

'Of course I'm all right. Why shouldn't I be?'

'*You* answer that. Here, you'd better sit down for a moment.'

Despite her bravado he had to lead her towards one of the wrought iron tables with its matching white chairs and she was forced to go with him. Just another cruel blow of fate. This man she had avoided like an unwelcome plague from the moment Aunt Elizabeth had welcomed him in the hall. She had been returning from the kitchen and Aunt Elizabeth had called to her delightedly to come meet Julie's cousin, Marsh McConnell. A swift glance had given her the impression of height and strength and dark features too strongly cast. He had a bold look about him, a look of freedom and challenge, like a pirate masquerading in elegant evening clothes. Worse, there was a frightening intelligence in his brilliant dark eyes. Jo knew she would recognise him again —anywhere. He was that kind of man. Smiling a conventional smile, and hardly aware of it, she still managed to convey to him her unnatural reaction. It saturated the atmosphere: sheer, primitive antagonism not unmixed with a little fear. This man was her enemy. Her look told him that plainly not only because he was part of her rival's world, but because of the way that he looked at her with an insolent challenge as unexpected as it was unprovoked. It seemed strange to her now that he should be the one to rescue her. His voice was at one with his appearance, dark and decisive with a decided hint of steel.

'Put your head down!' he said curtly. 'It might help.'

'I'm perfectly lucid, thank you. Goodness knows, there's nothing wrong with me.'

'Obviously there is. You were about to faint.'

'I wasn't!' she said angrily.

'Let it alone!' He bent her head forward, his fingers stabbing through her thick silky mane.

She wanted to slump right down on the grass, but he was ordering her to breathe deeply and after a few minutes she began to hate him so much she swung up her head. 'Are you usually so domineering?' she demanded.

'I don't suffer fools gladly!' His dark eyes slipped over her face and bare shoulders, ran down the length of her body, studied the lovely sea-green dress that matched her eyes but gave her no confidence. 'It's been something of an ordeal, hasn't it?'

'I don't know what you're talking about!' His words and his tone were so completely at odds, the singular lack of kindness had the effect of sending the adrenalin coursing through her veins, restoring her colour.

'Why do you women bother with play-acting?' he went on.

'We *love* it!'

For answer he caught hold of her chin, turning her head so she had to look towards the terrace. 'Go on, look at them. Get it out of your system.'

'How dare you!' She jerked her head away, a long silky black strand of her hair catching on the button on his sleeve.

'I can see the greed in your eyes!' he said, negligently loosening her hair.

'*Greed*—God!' she broke off, almost in tears. '*Grief.*'

'So I was right?'

Jo fell backwards, moaning softly. 'So you were testing me?'

'Yes.'

'Why would you want to be so cruel?'

'There's no simple answer. In this case it might be a kindness. What's the Jo short for—Joanne?'

'Josephine.'

Marsh seemed to find this amusing. 'I suppose you could upset an emperor at that!'

Jo had her eyes closed, her head thrown back for his insolent appraisal. 'I've known Blair all my life.'

'And you regard him as a brother?'

'I don't think this is any of your business.'

'Lady, it *is*! I'm all Julie has left in the way of a family and I think she needs a little help. I've heard about you.'

'Just a minute, you're going too fast!' She opened her eyes and they seemed to glow in the dark like a cat's.

'Really?' he drawled.

'Yes, really. What do you mean you've heard about me? Tell me before my patience runs out.'

'Let's say, beautiful lady, I'd heard about your black hair and your green eyes and the way you regarded Blair as your property.'

She was literally shaking with anger. 'You may not realise this, Mr Know-All McConnell, but Aunt Elizabeth, Blair's mother, very nearly raised me.'

'As the daughter she never had?'

'I love her dearly. And Uncle Joss. You should have made sure of your facts.'

'Oh, I always do that. I know they've been watching you pretty anxiously all evening.'

'So what?'

'Put their minds at rest. Find a man of your own.' She looked around her a little wildly, but he put a hard hand on her shoulder. 'Relax. You're a big girl now. You should be able to face up to facts.'

'I know I *hate* you!' she choked.

'You put a lot of feeling into that,' he observed. 'I wasn't sure you could spare any for anyone else but Julie's fiancé. Why don't we go up on the terrace and join them?'

She visibly recoiled from him. 'I couldn't dance with *you*!'

'But you will. You see, no one is going to hurt my cousin while I'm around. She's a very sweet, gentle girl and she needs a little protection from witches. Anyway, her life hasn't been all that easy.'

From somewhere she found a little mocking laugh. 'I find that hard to believe. I'd heard she was an heiress.'

'There are more important things than money.'

'Blair doesn't think so.'

'That was unforgivable!' he said harshly.

'So are you! Who are you to take me to task for anything? Why don't you go away and leave me alone.'

'So you can fascinate Julie's man? Fascinate me instead.'

'You're crazy!' she said, and stood up at once.

'Not at all!' He stood up to join her and though she was a tall girl she had quite a way to meet his eyes.

'Please tell me what this is all about?' she demanded.

'I have my reasons, Josephine. *Good* ones. I saw all the furtive little glances tonight. I'd never trust a woman with green eyes myself.'

'Would you trust any woman?' she asked scathingly.

'No. Not outside of Julie.'

'Then why don't you marry her yourself?'

'Obviously I don't think of her in that way. Anyway, how do you know I'm *not* married?'

'Give me some credit!'

'For what?'

'For knowing a married man when I see one.'

'Now this is interesting,' he drawled. 'What's the poor devil supposed to look like?'

'Not spoiling for a fight!' she said aggressively. 'A married man is usually more mellow, kinder, more tolerant. Understanding of women.'

'Oh, I understand them all right!' he returned dryly. 'I even understand your passion for Leighton.'

'You're a very straight shooter, aren't you?'

'When I have to be, and I have a very definite goal in mind—Julie's happiness. You strike me as pitiful. And much more—dangerous!'

Jo made a quick instinctive gesture that was never completed. He caught at her flying hand and pinned her wrist, holding it helpless against him. 'Cats usually fight with their claws, not the back of the hand. Don't you understand anything, you little fool?'

'I'd like you to let me go,' she said in a deadly kind of voice. '*Let go!*'

'I will when you come to your senses.'

'I haven't made a fool of myself up until now.'

'That's what I'm here for, to pull you back into line. You have to admit you were pretty badly shaken.'

'Perhaps I've reason to be!' she said bitterly.

'You mean Leighton is a cheat?'

He nearly threw her away from him and she fell back saying nothing. 'Well?'

It was a kind of compulsion to draw sympathy from even this very formidable man, but somehow Jo resisted the impulse, protective of Blair to the end. 'You came to an engagement party, didn't you?' she parried.

He seemed to relax. 'All right, then. Don't take it so hard. I guess we all run into an emotional crisis at some time in our lives. Leighton doesn't strike me as a rare prize, but he seems to know how to make Julie happy.'

'Brilliant!' she said acidly.

'Little bitch!'

'That's the really great thing about women! I don't think I can go back up there.'

'Why not?' Unexpectedly he tilted her chin. 'You're

the best looking woman at the party.'

'That's not such a big deal as you think!' She stared back at him, trying to retain her self-control. A panic of tears was just behind her eyes. He obviously didn't know it, but she felt badly injured for all her so-called beauty. Blair didn't want her. She might even have said it aloud, for he was looking down at her strangely, without the strong dash of contempt he had shown her up until now.

'For God's sake!' he burst out explosively, the man of steel. 'Why tear yourself to pieces like this? Come with me and forget your troubles.'

'You seem to forget I don't like you!'

'So what? I don't like you either, but I'm going to fight to keep you by my side. To the victor belong the spoils. Since we've been out here Leighton hasn't taken his eyes off this area. Why don't we give him something to think about?'

'You're mad!' she said, then checked in alarm, for he loomed towards her, pulling her into his arms, seeking her mouth and kissing it hard.

'*No!*' he warned her against her trapped mouth. 'You're as good as bound and tied. Make it look as if you're enjoying it. You want to save your reputation, don't you? It's a moonlit night and you're essentially a siren!'

Loathing was pulsing between them and an angry passion. Jo's heart was beating feverishly, unevenly, and the fragrance of gardenias was so heavy in the air the waxy blooms might have been crushed up between them. She was furious with Marsh, still madly in love with Blair, yet this man's sensual technique was crashing through her aversion in hot, swirling waves. He was holding her, kissing her with such intimacy that she could have killed him if she didn't feel like falling.

When he released her he was laughing softly. 'I somehow don't think you enjoyed that!'

'I don't like to associate with pirates.'

'I've tried every civilised means of stopping you from coming to pieces. What does a furious embrace matter? All anyone could say is: Lucky Jo, she can pick any man she likes!'

'You're not exactly my type!' she snapped.

'Thank God for that! Now are you coming back to the party? You look much better. Your eyes are sparkling and your mouth looks full and soft and thoroughly kissed.'

'You're very unusual, Mr McConnell. One of the world's outspoken souls.'

'Make it Marsh!'

She took her eyes from his face and powerful body. 'If you can put up with me for the rest of the evening the least I can do is put up with you.'

'There now!' he said mockingly, and laughed, a strangely attractive sound. His teeth were very white in his piratical dark face and Jo realised some women might find him extraordinarily exciting.

'Where do you come from?' she asked him. 'You don't seem to fit any ordinary background.'

'Don't you know?'

'Incredibly, no. I didn't even know you existed until a few hours ago.'

'When I'd heard all about you!' he jeered softly.

'From whom?'

'Eventually I'll tell you. Leave your hair alone, it looks fine. Don't ever cut it. Some man is going to want to strangle you with it.'

'You've got me badly miscast,' she said.

'I don't think so. If you're as sweet and demure as you're trying to make out you shouldn't have worn that dress. It's a show-stopper.'

'It's in perfectly good taste.'

'And it tells in a word that you've a very beautiful body.'

'Thank you. *Do* I thank you?'

'Don't turn those calculating green eyes on me.'

'You're the last creature on earth I could picture as a friend,' she said coldly.

'Since when have men and women been *friends*?'

'Blair was my friend!' she said baldly, and stopped.

'And you didn't win.'

'Who said I expected to? Your cousin Julie got him.'

'That much we know. Let's go up.' He took her arm and led her back across the lawn, and there was a kind of dangerous excitement in playing this part. It might even help her get through what remained of the night. The rosy glow of light from the terrace threw his profile into stark relief. It might have been a sculpture in bronze, very bold and strong. The forehead rounded and wide, nose and chin aggressive, the mouth moulded and very clearly defined, the head heavy and well shaped, covered in crisp black waves that would curl if left to grow just a fraction longer. Just the kind of man to set up vibrations.

'Well, what do you do?' Jo persisted, to calm herself. 'Background and so forth?'

'I have a property out West,' he uttered off-handedly. 'If you play your cards right I might even ask you out!'

'I won't come.'

She was suddenly under his black, brilliant scrutiny. 'What if I implore you, *Josephine*?'

'After tonight, I never want to see you again!'

'That's a nuisance!'

'And don't make fun of my name!'

'It's charming and it suits you—somehow!'

'What do you want to see me for?' she demanded.

'Oh, maybe to keep you safely out of the way.'

They had reached the terrace and without hesitation he took her in his arms, a very dominant kind of man. 'Simply behave as though you're enjoying yourself.'

Jo sighed and half rested against him. 'Do you like torturing women?'

'Just a moment—I don't remember any other woman complaining!'

'I suppose it's your bank balance!'

'I'll tell you when the time comes!' His arm tightened around her and he guided her very expertly towards the other dancers. 'Breathe deeply. It's great for jittery nerves!'

'Then there's always the chance you'll crush me. Your grip is defying me to escape.'

'In another minute you'll be glad of it.'

She didn't see them until a soft voice asked directly behind her shoulder:

'Enjoying yourselves, you two?'

Jo could feel her colour ebb away, but somehow she was turning around to return Julie's rather tentative smile. Her glance shifted to Blair for a split second and she wanted to cry. Whether this was an engagement party or not she knew him too well not to miss the masked hostility in his expression. His amber eyes were piercing her face, and she couldn't begin to understand it. He looked jealous and far from pleased, this seducer of women. It didn't make sense. Through a daze she heard Marsh McConnell make some particularly hypo-critical remark about enjoying himself immensely, then he was steering her away determinedly. Jo was shaking with the strain. She should have been thanking him, but she could only think of Blair as he had been with the sun on his hair and his skin, the way he had of fitting all of her moods. This man was too strongly masculine, too blunt and forceful, too cruelly mocking, yet the slender bones of her body seemed to melt against him as though his hard powerful body was lending her strength.

'Good girl!' he murmured, bending his dark head over her.

'I can't take it any more,' she said shakily.

'You're doing just fine.'

She lifted her head at this unexpected approval and

outrageously, in front of a dozen watching eyes, he brushed her mouth with his own. 'That's for you, you poor little devil!'

'Go to hell!' she returned, equally quiet. 'I'm not grateful for any of this.'

'You ought to be, but then you're very spoiled.'

'And you're as clever as three foxes. Who filled your ears with tales of me?'

'What matters is I took good notice. Here comes Leighton to switch partners and I won't let him.'

She shuddered in violent reaction and his black eyes narrowed dangerously. 'Let's pretend I'm out to win your gorgeous hand.'

'You're taking the wrong road.'

'Let's wait and see what happens!'

In the end, Julie defeated him, speaking directly to him, her voice affectionate and confident. 'Marsh, I haven't danced with you all evening!'

'Then we'll have to change that this minute. I've never seen you look prettier.'

It was more than Jo felt she should bear, but Julie was smiling at her like a friendly little girl, her blue eyes just a little fussed. 'You don't mind, do you, Jo?'

'Of course not. I was getting a little tired anyway!'

'*Lovely!*' Marsh McConnell commented satirically.

'You know what I mean!' Her green gaze hit his hard.

'Let me get something to revive you!' Blair released his fiancée and caught at Jo's hand, twisting it painfully. 'Jo's built for speed, not for stamina. She was like that as a little girl!'

Julie gave rather a feverish little laugh and pressed close to her cousin's tall, rangy body. 'Blair told me all about you, Jo. I know we're going to be friends!'

'Why not?' she returned flippantly. 'I'll tell you my side!'

'Behave yourself, Jo!' Blair said, and laughed, his amber eyes full of a vaguely malicious glitter.

A steady drift of dancers were coming out of the house and Marsh looked at Jo with black, challenging eyes. 'Don't go too far away!'

'I won't, I promise.'

This seemed to satisfy Julie, for she laughed softly and turned her slight, petite body into her cousin's arms, staring up at him and already plying him with questions.

'Let's get out of here!' Blair muttered beneath his breath.

'I've nothing to say to you.'

'It would be just like you to create a scandal. Don't do it here.'

The effrontery and unfairness of this almost took her breath away, and he took advantage of the moment to turn her back towards the floodlit garden where a few couples were strolling leisurely. Despite herself, her bones were melting at his touch. 'Please, Blair. You won't be able to do this now you're very nearly a married man.'

'Who the hell does he think he is?' he growled.

'Marsh McConnell?'

'What's he after, a quick affair?'

In her anger she was stammering. 'Honestly, Blair, you'll never cease to surprise me. You've demonstrated more than adequately that you don't care what I do with the rest of my life.'

'Keep your voice down!' he muttered angrily.

'Why, so you can keep up this ghastly pretence?'

'I care about her,' he said almost petulantly.

'God, I hope so. He'll kill you if you don't.'

'And what's it to him?'

'In his own words, he's all the family she's got. *You* know the story, I don't. You just sprang it on us all. Your mother is reeling from the shock!'

'Mother's all right!' he said carelessly, adored and indulged from his very first breath. 'I'd much rather it were *you*, Jo, but you can't help me. Try to understand.'

'I'm sorry I can't!' she said, leaden with misery. 'Only last week you told me you loved me.'

'I haven't changed!'

He tried to take her hands, but she drew back from him violently. 'Am I supposed to be grateful for that? I trusted you with my life. Now you calmly bring Julie, a stranger, into our lives and get your mother to throw a big engagement party. There doesn't seem any excuse or pardon for your behaviour. What's this to be, a marriage of convenience? I thought they'd gone out of style?'

'They'll never go out of style,' he answered cynically. 'There's too much to be gained. I'm ambitious, Jo. Julie can help me, and she's a sweet little thing. She knows how to dress and she'll make a nice little bit of window-dressing. Life with Julie won't be any hardship, and it won't affect us!'

Jo shook her head helplessly, utterly dismayed at his reasoning. 'You can't really mean this, Blair. I can't work with you now. You must realise that.'

He turned and faced her, a slim, very elegant man and for one moment a bitter anger blazed in his eyes. 'I *know* you, Jo. There's more passion in your little finger than Julie's whole body. She's nearly sexless compared to you.'

'But this is cruel! You can't go into a marriage feeling like that. She has some rights too. She deserves someone who loves her. She's madly in love with you!'

'She'll never know the difference!' Blair looked back at her steadily and his whole attitude was reflected in his amber eyes.

'I don't suppose she will!' Jo returned in a low voice.

'So you see, darling, I haven't abandoned you. How could I? You and I are a team. You're necessary to the business. You're a talented designer and I've big plans for expansion. With some real money behind me I could branch out into new markets. Leighton & Associates of Melbourne—we could make it a big name. All the clients like you and you're a terrific asset with the men.'

'I can't be when the man I love is going to marry someone else.'

'Don't be a drivelling idiot, darling. My marriage will be a business arrangement like everything else.'

'You mean you don't intend to share the same bed?'

'I very much doubt if I could get out of that. I mean, after all, the price has to be paid.'

'You sound amused!' she said incredulously.

'I wish it was catching. Don't make any grand gestures that could explode in your face. Stay with me, love. What do you say?'

She didn't reply immediately because the tears of pain and frustration weren't very far away, but eventually she said in a low, toneless voice. 'I thought we were doing pretty well as we were. Isn't half the enjoyment in life forging ahead under your own steam, being your own man? Retaining your integrity, I'm trying to say. You started the business on your own. Why not go on from there?'

'You're talking nonsense, Jo!' said Blair with the faintly crooked little smile that usually wrung her heart. 'A little backing from Julie will be equal to ten years of hard work. I want what I want, *now*!'

'Are you so sure she's prepared to part with her money?' Jo asked from the depths of her wretchedness.

'She knows I'm ambitious. She admires that very thing in me. Don't worry about Julie. She's not your problem.'

Her eyes travelled over the familiar outline of his face and body. He was no taller than she was in high heels and their eyes were level. 'Have you spoken to your mother like this?' she demanded.

'Don't be a little fool, and don't go trying to make trouble. Mother won't believe you. I'm her golden-haired boy!'

'Yes, you are!' she said simply. 'Her only son, her only child. I can't think now who you take after. Both of them are so wonderful, Aunt Elizabeth and Uncle Joss.'

'They were very good to you.'

'I know that. Father meant well, but I was always an unpleasant reminder that my mother chose to leave him.'

'Small wonder! These academic types are a crashing bore. All they know is their particular subject. Anyway, your father's dead now. You take things too hard, Jo. You've always had an obsessive kind of feeling for me.'

'You mean I loved you!' she said, like a requiem.

'You still love me!' he said urgently. 'And I can prove it right now!'

'Touch me and I'll scream!' The intensity of her rejection astonished her. This was Blair, the man she loved.

'Of course you will, dear!' His long fingers circled her wrist. 'I can feel your pulse, and it's in a flutter of panic. I want you so much I can hardly keep my hands off you.'

'It might be a good thing if you did from now on, and if you think I'm bluffing about the scream . . .'

'Jo!' he said carefully, but unlocked her wrist.

She rubbed it, trying to quiet her mind. 'I won't be dishonoured, Blair. It's an old-fashioned word, but that's what I mean. I'm an old-fashioned girl.'

'Incredibly you are!' he agreed. 'You've been silly about a lot of things when we could have been luxuriating in what we had!'

'You selfish swine!' she said into the darkness.

'Don't deny the demands of your own body, Jo. You're a passionate woman and you're living in a world of change.'

'Not for the better. Not in lots of ways. Anyway you never loved me, I can see that now. No one could inflict gross pain on the woman he loved. The wanting is physical. There's not another thing else.'

Blair lit a cigarette and said in a flat, even voice, 'Don't sound so humble, Jo, it doesn't suit you. You're not only beautiful, you're clever. I'm just trying to make you understand what kind of a man I am. I want a completely free hand to build up my business. Given that, I'll expand and triple our turnover in the first year. You're a highly competent and gifted designer, and I want you on my team.'

'I'm finding myself another job tomorrow,' she retorted.

'You won't get any reference from me!'

'Oh yes, I know what you'd do. Now that I really allow myself to think of it, you've done one or two underhand things.'

'Like every business man. Listen, Jo, you can't do this to me. I have to go interstate tomorrow, as you very well know. Someone has to be in the shop. Besides, what would the parents think, let alone the clients?'

'I can't worry about that now,' she shrugged. 'In the end I *must* leave you. You've made my position untenable.'

'Darling, I want to kiss you!' he said, stubbing out his cigarette.

'I'll scream so fast I'll crack the glasses!'

'Give yourself a little time to settle down. I'm telling you nothing has changed between us.'

Jo bit her bottom lip so hard she drew blood. 'You really mean it, don't you?'

'Yes.'

'I don't know you at all. Your ears are faintly pointed like a satyr's!'

'And you're able to tell from that what sort of man I am?' Blair smiled at her then, the old familiar crooked smile, his amber eyes startlingly bright under his hooded lids. 'Remember Mrs McConnell?'

'Why, of course!' she answered, off balance with the abrupt change of subject.

'Marsh McConnell's mother!'

'Well, really!' Jo was so shocked she almost felt like laughing hysterically.

'That's where I met Julie, at her aunt's. Didn't you ever wonder why I put you off that job? One of our biggest up to date. Julie's parents were killed in a car crash when she was about twelve and she went to live with her grandparents. You've surely heard of Caldwell's Wines? Old Caldwell was Julie's grandad, also McConnell's. Both of them benefited considerably from his estate along with the rest of the clan, but I understand from Julie that neither McConnell nor his mother had need of it. He's in the big time himself—some property out West. They've even found valuable mineral deposits on his land. That's another thing with these damned millionaires, money just comes to them. I've had to work hard. Julie looks on him as some kind of Big Brother!'

'If you know that, why show your antagonism?'

'I don't like him and I don't want him taking an interest in you. You're *mine*!'

Jo gave a tired smile. 'That's where you're making a fatal mistake. We never did have that weekend away, and I'm not sharing you with a wife.'

Blair threw up both hands, supremely confident. 'Julie's pretty dumb under that sweetness.'

'Don't mistake her blind love for you as stupidity!'

'She won't learn that I don't love her from me!'

Jo turned abruptly, the light catching the brilliant sheen of her dress. 'I'm going back inside, Blair. I've had enough. What you're intending is despicable and it will bring you sorrow.'

'Is that supposed to be funny?' A wave of colour ran up his lean cheeks.

'Not at all. I've never been more serious in my life. As far as I'm concerned you stabbed me in the back—a coward's way out!'

'Jo, for God's sake,' he begged, 'be a little kind to me. I can't expect you to congratulate me even when I intend that you share in my good fortune.'

'Put it out of your thoughts!' she said, her head flung back proudly. 'I'm going absent from tomorrow!'

'No,' he said, and put out his hand to touch her. 'One of the best things about you is your loyalty. You know I have to make this trip. All my appointments have been set up. I have manufacturers to meet. You can't walk out on me, Jo. I've made you what you are. In time I could set you up as a partner. I told you I've got plans. We could expand into the commercial sector, take on more staff—one or two designers with flair. Professionals of course. Can't you see where we could go?'

'I'm sorry, Blair!' The touch of his skin against hers was making her weaken. 'I can't kill what I feel for you and I can't work for you feeling this way. It wouldn't be right!'

'I can't talk to you here!' he said rapidly. 'Julie is the most casual girl in the world. She believes everything I say.'

'So did I,' said Jo bitterly. 'I know you're brilliant, I know you're going to make a big name for yourself. I wish you and your Julie all the luck in the world— particularly Julie. I'm beginning to feel sorry for her.'

'Don't feel sorry for Julie,' he said savagely. 'She has me!'

'You can't imagine what that sounds like!'

She saw his gaze wandering all over her. The face he had kissed, the curve of her breast. He had wanted so much of her and God knows in time she might have given it to him. 'Oh, Blair!' she sighed, and the hot tears sprang into her eyes.

'Cry, darling, if you want to. You're nearly driving me crazy. Think this thing out. Nothing has really changed. We'll still be together, only this time I'll have the money to set me free!'

'I loved you,' she said brokenly.

'It can't be, Jo!' he said almost despairingly. 'I *can't* marry you, but it's no real cause for unhappiness. Don't

be so bloody simple-minded. I'll always look after you.
We'll always be together.'

'Oh yes! Always a mistress, never a wife. I want a life
of my own, don't you know? A home. Children. I'm
twenty-five years old.'

'Then it's about time you learnt the ways of the world.'

'The ways of men, don't you mean? This isn't getting
us anywhere.'

Her hair fell like black satin against the curve of her
cheek and he reached out a hand and ran it along the
thick shining wave in a remembered gesture. 'Please say
you'll help me, Jo. I can't trust anyone else. No one
knows the business like you do and Olive is only good
for the donkey-work.'

'How long do you expect to be away?'

'Possibly the week. I can't rush anything.'

'All right, Blair,' she sighed, 'I'll stay until then. As
you say, you've taught me a lot.'

'I want to teach you so much more. I'm going to be
your lover.' He held up her face forcibly, studying the
flawless, light-olive skin, and marvellous bones, the
treacherously passionate mouth, trembling now, and he
cried out in intense irritation. 'For God's sake, Jo, why
spoil everything now?'

'There's honour, you know!'

'You're mad. Let me see you tonight, after they've all
gone home. Damn them to hell!'

'Your Julie is coming very quickly across the lawn,' Jo
observed. 'She's not as stupid as you think.'

'I need a drink!' he said tonelessly. 'All Julie touches
is iced orange juice. How's that for Caldwell's grand-
daughter?'

'You're a heartless monster! She looks like a very nice
girl.'

'How generous you are, Jo, to your rival.'

'At least I can understand her,' said Jo. 'I was stupidly
in love with you too!'

He threw a quick look at her as though she was about to revenge herself on him. 'Smile, for God's sake. You look as moody as hell!'

'Oh? Marsh told me I was the best looking woman at the party.'

'Let him get back to his splendid estate!' Blair returned violently. 'We don't want him here.'

Julie was almost upon them. It didn't seem possible she wouldn't sense the electric tension in the air. She looked as pretty and delicate as a pink azalea in her lovely chiffon dress, floating around her, her soft curls springing back from her childishly round forehead. She looked so defenceless, so innocent of malice or duplicity, Jo couldn't blame her for anything. Blair was totally to blame and all three of them were no more than figures in a very small drama.

Blair gave his winning crooked smile and threw out an arm. 'Come here to me, darling!'

Julia ran to him on small, silver sandalled feet, a Dresden figure from the tip of her primrose curls to her pearly-lacquered toes. She bore no resemblance whatever to the McConnells, mother and son. Jo remembered Cybill McConnell as a very striking-looking woman, a brunette, with immense self-assurance. Julie, for a rich girl, was extraordinarily unassuming and demure. She even glanced at Jo with a hint of apology.

'I got lonely. I hope I'm not interrupting?'

'How could you?' Jo returned as pleasantly as she could.

Blair dropped a kiss on Julie's pink and white skin as though thirsting for the touch of it. 'Jo and I have been discussing business as usual. You'll get used to it, baby. I'm flying interstate tomorrow, as you know. Jo's in charge while I'm away!'

'You must be very clever, Jo!' Julie said with what seemed to be genuine admiration, nestling in to Blair's side with a wide-eyed stare.

'Years of study!' Jo said lightly. 'Blair's the brilliant one!'

'Yes, darling!' Julie looked up at him and gave a soft laugh. 'Everyone tells me that. I'm so proud of you.'

'I'm going to get you in and explain everything to you.'

'Maybe *I* can do that!' The impulse to make that sardonic suggestion mastered Jo for an instant, and Blair's smooth handsome face betrayed a flicker of anxiety.

'I must say that's very nice of you, Jo. I want you two girls to be friends. But you must promise to leave all the difficult little bits to me.'

Julie was gazing raptly at him as though the sun rose and set on his thin, elegant face. 'I'm not in the least clever.'

'I love you!' he said with lazy sensuality, and she blushed deeply like a rose.

Jo's reserves were running out. 'I've just learnt this minute that Mrs McConnell is your aunt. I admired her enormously. Her taste is superb—a very cultivated lady.'

Julie smiled and said happily, 'It was Aunt Cybill who brought Blair and me together. I'll always bless her for that. She's my very favourite aunt, just as Marsh has made himself my big brother!'

'Make that capitals!' Jo commented, noticeably sharp.

'He's obviously smitten with you, Jo,' Julie went on. 'Marsh is used to having women fight over him. You have reason to be gratified with his attention!' Julie looked at her with some surprise.

'Oh, I am!' Jo's deeply moulded mouth curved downwards. 'If you'll excuse me, I think I'll go and have an orange drink!'

Blair glanced at her with a faint anger in his eyes, then he murmured to his fiancée with exquisite indulgence, 'Are you going to permit yourself one little drink, precious girl?'

'I suppose it's permissible at one's own engagement party!'

'As I live and breathe!' said Jo.

Julie for some reason began to fidget with a chiffon fold of her dress. 'I really came down to tell you some of our guests are wanting to get away. We'd better go back to the house. Come back with us, Jo. Marsh is expecting you.'

'I'd be delighted. It's time someone told me what's the Marsh short for—or is that it?'

'He was christened James Marshall McConnell. The Marshall is a family name!'

'Oh, I thought he might have been the local sheriff as well as everything else.'

'Jo, you're outrageous!' Blair folded his arm around her waist, and careless of the cruelty of it fitted both girls to his side, strolling back to the terrace with them like the practised actor he was. His intention of presenting a united front was understandable, but his callousness was making Jo feel mildly hysterical. For the moment she was trapped at his side, an unwilling party to this deception. She knew that once inside the house again Marsh McConnell would come to claim her for his own reasons and surprisingly she experienced a deep sense of relief. It was preferable to have the clean thrust of his mockery than Blair's fingers subtly pressing into the curve of her waist.

Almost at once they could see the crowd had begun to thin out except for a younger group still dancing, and there was Aunt Elizabeth, beautifully turned out in an outfit made up to her son's design, calling out to them:

'Come up, my dears! It's been a wonderful party, but remember it's a work day tomorrow. Mary and Alex are wanting to leave!'

'Oh, we must see them off!' Julie gave a little joyful spirt. 'You come too, Jo!' she added kindly, and it sounded as if she meant it.

Jo didn't answer. She was too bewildered and stricken to warm to Julie and she wasn't at all sure she was as artless as she seemed. She glanced up then and saw Marsh McConnell leaning over the balcony staring down at them—no doubt admiring the picture they made: Blair, shiningly fair and elegant between the two girls, who couldn't have presented a better foil for each other. Julie, almost doll-like in her lack of inches, a fragile study in pastels. Jo, with her beautiful, vivid face above an equally beautiful long-stemmed body. It would be very hard indeed to feel sympathy for a girl who carried herself so proudly and had so many apparent assets. She didn't need to get nearer to hear his brain ticking over, turning out data like a computer. Julie's happiness couldn't be guaranteed with a girl like Jo around. Three-cornered love was a jungle where no one was safe!

CHAPTER TWO

WHEN Jo came down to breakfast, make-up covered her telling pallor. She had passed a miserable night with bouts of crying, accompanied by dreams, like cruel jokes, where Blair held her in his arms and swore he would never let her go. She couldn't break free of them, only to weep and lament that she had ever believed him and handed her heart to him on a plate. She had gone to bed with a splitting headache and after all that crying it had gathered strength to plague her again. She couldn't wait for a cup of strong black coffee to revive her. The pity was, and quite unavoidable, that she had to stay the night to help Aunt Elizabeth tidy up until the cleaning woman came in this morning. It was useless to bemoan that she didn't have the privacy of her own apartment. When one was down, one was very much down, and Aunt Elizabeth especially would be still full of talk about Julie and the party. Of Uncle Joss she was not so sure. His grave inquiring glance saw far too much. It was just as well Blair had taken the early morning flight; she couldn't have faced him and seen the inevitable understanding in Uncle Joss's quiet face.

Characteristically, even in the worst circumstances, she was beautifully dressed and made up, and her mirror proclaimed her valiant efforts. She looked totally female and a chic businesswoman. It was better by far to try and act normally than give way to a deepening feeling that nothing had importance any more. It was time to face reality. What she wanted out of life she wasn't going to get. The Blair she had loved simply didn't exist beyond her blind imaginings. The way he had treated her, the callous way he spoke of the girl he was marrying, proved beyond a doubt that this cross she was bearing was really a blessing in disguise. In time her errant heart would accept her mind's evaluation. She had just over an hour to get to the shop. It was Olive's morning off, so she couldn't afford to be late. Now even the work she loved was going to be taken from her. Very few of the designers around the city had Blair's stamp of genius. He had established himself very firmly, for all his belittling his own achievements.

Jo looked around her cautiously and heard Aunt Elizabeth singing softly to herself in the kitchen. Her happiness and pride in her son had made her quite beautiful last night. Jo didn't go into her as she normally would have done, but moved through the big open-plan living/dining room out to the informal sun room where the first meal of the day was taken. Blair had redecorated it not so long ago and his flair could be seen immediately, casually sophisticated and a beautiful place to start the day.

Uncle Joss, a public servant and almost at retiring age was seated with his back to her, the paper almost up to his nose nearly toppling his teacup.

'Hi!' she said in a voice she reserved for him but didn't know it.

'Good morning, Jo!' He glanced up at her with unfeigned pleasure and began to fold up his newspaper. 'I was hoping you'd come down and join me. I've got a few minutes before I have to go.'

She bent down and kissed his cheek, pressing his shoulders. 'You look none the worse for wear!'

'Grand party, wasn't it?'

'Marvellous!' said Jo, sinking into a chair facing the garden. It was from his father that Blair had inherited his chiselled features and his artistic impulses. The garden was Joss Leighton's own brand of artistic perfection. It was sheer magic and truly inspired, with landscaping and surprise corners and conifers standing like sentinels over the beautifully groomed lawns and massed displays of flowers.

'It introduced Julie to all our friends. I know we've thanked you before, Jo, for the big part you played in making it a success. Elizabeth needed all your help and she's very grateful. I want to thank you again. You're a fine girl—too good for most men!'

'Don't say that, dear!' she said wryly. 'I want to get married and you sound like I might frighten them off.'

He put his cup down and reached out a hand to her covering hers with his own. 'Don't, Jo. We're good friends. I know how you feel—after all these years I'd have to. Believe me, you'll get over it. I love Blair. He's my son, but he's not good enough for you!'

'Please, Uncle Joss!' she said raggedly. 'You'll make me cry and that will ruin my make-up. I have to get to work.'

'You don't have to, you know!' he said quietly. 'Let Blair look after his own affairs. He thinks he knows how and he's quite ruthless about using people. I'm not blind to his faults just because I'm his father. Listen, before Elizabeth comes, I have a little money. I think you deserve a holiday. Just between the two of us. I'm very fond of you, Jo. You're the daughter we never had. Blair has acted badly, hasn't he? Made you some promises?'

'No, Uncle Joss.'

'Then why won't you look at me? You can tell me the truth!' Joss Leighton gave a grim laugh. 'I'm on your side, child. Liz has ruined the boy—I've told her often enough. He wants every last little thing to fall into his hands.'

'He's quite brilliant, Uncle Joss!' she pointed out because she had to. 'Everyone thinks very highly of him—craftsmen, manufacturers, builders, architects, clients. Blair will go far!'

'I did want him to get there under his own steam.

But he hungers after money, all the things it can buy him.'

'He's not alone there. You mustn't say anything like this to Aunt Elizabeth.'

'Do you think she'd listen?' he asked gently. 'Blair can do no wrong in his mother's eyes!'

'It would do no good anyway. Julie seems a very nice girl. I don't think she'll be too demanding. Blair wouldn't want that. It will work out. I want it too— *terribly*!'

'Why, dear?'

She blinked away the incipient tears and laughed nervously. 'Maybe it's you I love after all. Blair looks very much like you, but without your backbone. Oh, I'm sorry . . .'

'It's all right!' He folded his napkin neatly. 'Now quickly, before Elizabeth comes in with your breakfast —she's on top of the world, by the way—what about that holiday? A trip somewhere. I don't think it would be a good idea to stay with Blair!'

'I told him I'd go in until the end of the week!'

'I bet he absolutely insisted!' A deep frown ran between his brows.

'That's reasonable. There are many things to attend to. He got away on time?'

'I didn't see him. His mother saw him off. In some ways I'm deeply disappointed in my son!' Joss Leighton's still bright amber eyes looked beyond them to the garden. 'What about a small statue to set off the climbing roses?'

'I think it would be charming. I'll find you one.'

'Good girl. *My* girl. You're too forgiving, Jo!'

'What else is there?' she asked with false calm. 'I saw what bitterness did to my father!'

'Ah yes!' Joss Leighton glanced at her downcast face. 'Charles was a strange man and he deprived himself of the incomparable joy of having a beautiful, loving daughter. Don't let the life go out of you, Jo. Your spirit is unique. Do you really think little Julie will be able to handle my son?'

Jo couldn't answer at once. Her hand began to shake and Joss Leighton looked down at her glossy black head, the hair fallen forward protectively, as shiny as a magpie's wing. 'Jo dear, I'm sorry! What an unthinking old fool I am!'

There was so much pain in his voice, this more than anything else lent Jo a measure of control. She drew a sharp breath and looked up, her green eyes brilliant with unshed tears like a leaf after rain. 'I think she loves him so much she'll ask little in return. I hope for her sake this is so.'

'Incredible!' Blair's father exclaimed. 'I suppose the gossips are already saying he's marrying her for her money!'

'She's very pretty, Uncle Joss. No one could deny that.'

'She's not a patch on you in any way.'

'You're prejudiced. Anyway, she has a family.'

'Yes ... that McConnell chap! I liked him, but I wouldn't want to do anything to cross him. He's very fond of Julie, I understand!'

'Something of a watchdog!' she said dryly.

Joss looked at her searchingly and saw the way her lovely, generous mouth tightened and her hands clenched on the table. 'Didn't you like him? You seemed to be inseparable for the latter part of the evening!'

'He might sweep plenty of women off their feet, but not me!' Jo said violently when she was supposed to be indifferent. 'His kind of man is quite foreign to me.'

'Oh, I thought you made a very handsome couple.'

'You're joking!'

'No, I'm not. Marsh McConnell is a very striking man!'

'I thought him flamboyant!'

'Why? Because he's no fool and the very opposite to Blair. That alone, I suppose, would create an antagonism!'

'I won't say this to anyone else,' said Jo, 'but my heart is broken. I don't expect it to mend easily. I'm like that!'

A great tenderness welled up in Joss Leighton's kindly eyes. 'Give yourself a little time, Jo. Your promise is enormous!'

'I'm twenty-five, Uncle Joss.'

'And you've decided that's on the shelf?'

'You know my weakness. I'm one-track!'

'There's a limit to everything, Jo,' he said thoughtfully. 'You gave your heart away as a schoolgirl. You're a woman now, time to ask yourself a few questions. We're still good friends, aren't we?'

'We're family, Uncle Joss,' she said simply. 'I love you far more than I ever did my poor tormented father. Not that he wanted my love.'

'And you've such a lot to give. Let me make you a present of this trip. What about England? You'd love that, you've always wanted to go. This is Jubilee Year. What better time?'

She smiled and her lips quivered. 'That's very dear of you, Uncle Joss, but I know perfectly well you're saving for that world trip. I would never take it off you. It's not so much to fly to London these days. I really do have the money—I spend a great deal on clothes; I have to. It's part of the image and Blair expects it. But thank you for thinking of me. It's just like you!'

'The matter's not closed. I have quite a comfortable nest-egg set aside, and there's all my superannuation. Here comes Elizabeth. Courage, dear, I know she's going to try you in her maternal pride. Mothers wear blinkers!'

'You're leaving, then?' Jo looked up at him anxiously.

'I must, my dear. Public servants are not allowed to be late. Ah, Elizabeth dear. I'm off now. Here's Jo bright and shining and waiting for her breakfast. You'll have to hurry, Jo, if you want to make it to the shop on time!'

'Good morning, dear!' Aunt Elizabeth smiled brightly at Jo and bent over the laden breakfast trolley. She was a pretty, very earnest-looking little woman with fair hair streaked with silver, a pleasantly rounded figure and a petal soft skin.

'Here, let me take that!' Jo got up with swift grace, took hold of the trolley and wheeled it right up to the table. She turned back just in time to see Aunt Elizabeth and Uncle Joss exchange a tender, loving peck.

'What about lunch one day through the week, Jo?' said Joss, raising one eyebrow just like his son.

'That will be lovely, Uncle Joss. I'll ring you.'

'Fine. I'll keep myself free. Well, girls, I must be off. Take care!'

They chorused their goodbyes and Jo returned to her chair while Aunt Elizabeth sank into her husband's vacant seat. 'I wish you didn't have to go to work today, dear. I feel like a good old natter. I've been up so early. Blair got away before seven!'

'You don't look in the least tired,' Jo assured her. 'You look terrific.'

Aunt Elizabeth's high spirits were in complete contrast to the sickening lurch in Jo's stomach. 'I *feel* it!' she said. 'There, eat up like a good girl. Bacon and eggs, plenty of protein to keep you going until lunch time. I couldn't get Blair to touch a bite. He was a cross old bear this morning. I've made a pot of tea. I'll join you. You really should change over from coffee to tea, Jo. It's better for you and so much nicer. I always say there's nothing in this world like a good cuppa!'

'It's getting to be an extravagance these days, with rising prices!' Jo said dryly.

'Don't be sarcastic, my girl. It's cheaper than splitting a bottle of champagne—we did enough of that last night. You look lovely, dear!' A long glance of approval, exactly as usual. 'That's a beautiful suit. White is your colour, with your lovely tan!'

'You're on top of the world, aren't you?' Jo commented.

'I tell you I *am*! The funny thing was Blair was as irritable as blazes.'

'You told me before!' Jo said vaguely.

'You know how he is first thing in the morning—utterly antisocial. Of course he had very little sleep. It was very late by the time he got Julie home and then back to the house. My poor darling! He really works too hard!'

'I feel somewhat like that myself!'

'That's just what I mean. You're so clever, both of you. Blair did marvels with this room. I was so proud of the house last night. One would scarcely recognise it from the house we bought. Blair is a genius!'

'He thinks so too, incidentally!'

'Naughty, darling. Who's the one who has given him so much encouragement?'

'I only did it to get a job!'

Aunt Elizabeth laughed with overwhelming good humour and sipped at her tea. "What do you think of Julie?'

Jo tried very doggedly for a smile. 'A very sweet girl.'

'I thought so too. Not very stimulating, perhaps?'

'Give her a chance. She's rather shy and she's just getting to know us!'

'Lord, yes—I mean—' Elizabeth suddenly whipped out her glasses and planted them on her small tilted nose. 'Look, darling, you're the closest thing to a daughter I've got. Joss never has been one for a gossip and I wouldn't say it to anyone else—' Her myopic blue eyes searched Jo's face very earnestly. 'Blair is so very special—too special perhaps for his own good. Julie is a dear girl. I could come to love her. I just want a little reassurance. Blair was really so ... querulous, is that the word? this morning!'

'You ought to do something about those moods of his!' Jo returned, apparently idly.

'I mean to, but I love him so much and he's so good for so much of the time. All interesting, clever people are temperamental.'

'You never made the same allowances for me!'

'Now, dear, you're a female. Women just have to behave!'

'I really have to leave in a few minutes, Aunty dear. But fire away ...'

'Julie struck me as somewhat...' Aunt Elizabeth mused.

'I know what you mean!' Jo said quickly, feeling trapped in a closet. 'I'm sure she's a little different when they're on their own. It takes time to adjust, and women learn fast!'

'That they do!' Elizabeth laughed. 'He usually sweeps me up and kisses me, but he didn't even do that!'

'All right, girl, face facts. He had to catch a plane!'

'Of course, I ought to realise that. You're good for me, Jo. Don't think I'm criticising the child. It's obvious she's head over heels in love with my son. It shines right out of her eyes—very touching, really. I was wondering if he was ever going to make me a grandmother!'

Jo forced a comment, feeling ill and pathetic. 'Why else does anyone get married? There's no real case for not having a family!'

'You liked her, didn't you, Jo?' Aunt Elizabeth asked humbly, and Jo realised she still needed reassurance. No girl was too good for Blair. 'Your opinion is very important to me. Sometimes I think you're a lot smarter than I am!'

Jo swallowed her coffee very hot, scalding her throat. The first couple of words came out as a groan. 'What little I've seen, I like. She's pretty, she's intelligent. Her background is excellent. All of us may even be privileged to visit the McConnell family seat. Where is it, by the way?'

'Why don't you ask him?' Impish blue eyes roved Jo's face. 'He's a very attractive man!'

'Too damned good to be true!'

'You *didn't* like him?' Aunt Elizabeth asked in astonishment. 'You must have been fighting yourself last night!'

'*He* was pressing it, dear!'

'None of us are getting any younger, Jo. If I were you I'd grab him!'

'That's loose talk!' Jo finished off her meal quickly and stood up. 'Sorry to leave you, dear, but I must fly. You wouldn't like me to neglect the business. If you're going to look like that I'll give you some news. I did find Marsh McConnell attractive, but maybe a wee bit overwhelming!'

'A shame to waste it on just one woman. Make sure you're the lucky one, and that's good advice. He's just the man to sweep a woman off her feet!'

'You romantic, you!' scolded Jo.

'Yes, I am. Nothing complicated for me, just a knight on a white charger!' She put out a hand and grasped Jo's. 'Thank you, darling, for all the help. Only you and Blair are so like brother and sister I might have wished to keep you permanently in the family.'

Jo shook back her glossy black hair. 'Now who said you're not going to do that?'

'You'll go off and leave me!' For a second there was real concern in the powder blue eyes. 'I worry about you, Jo. About your happiness. You're a very beautiful girl. You should be married!'

'I mean to!' Jo said wryly. 'Maybe beautiful girls frighten men off?'

'You're so witty too!'

'Is that another black mark?'

'Of course not, dear. That's just fine. You'll make some man an absolutely wonderful wife!'

'Thank you, and I love you very much!' Jo turned away to touch up her lipstick. Her hands were shaking, but Aunt Elizabeth had her back to her.

'I hope Blair's feeling better. He said he'd ring me from Sydney. He was so nervy I just wish he could have curled up quietly and had a few more hours' sleep!'

Jo turned back casually, thinking the blush was standing out on her cheeks. 'Don't worry about him. He soon gets over his little fits of temperament. Make him apologise!'

'I mean to, but you know how it is!'

'Mrs Lacey coming in this morning?'

'Yes, I've just been talking to her. She's going to do everything.'

Jo lent down and kissed the soft, scented cheek. 'That was some celebration, Mrs Leighton!'

Aunt Elizabeth patted her hand. 'Just you wait until the wedding! You'll make a lovely bridesmaid!'

Jo stepped back so quickly she banged into the open door. 'I don't think so, darling. I'm too tall. Julie will want to ask her own friends!'

'She certainly won't!' Elizabeth turned a bright pink. 'Not *all* of them, anyway. With you and Blair so close it's only right you should be one of the bridesmaids!'

'Don't push it, dear. Just as long as he's happy!' It was an effort to smile, but Aunt Elizabeth didn't return the smile. She was shut in on her thoughts.

'She *is* tiny!'

'Your size!' Jo pointed out. 'They say men marry their mothers. You and Julie are both fair and petite!'

'I mean to bring this up myself with Julie. We could arrange it so you stood on the outside!'

Jo closed her eyes. 'Sorry, love, I have to go!' She bent and picked up her handbag, so upset she actually wanted to laugh right out loud. It might ease the tight clamp around her heart. There was even a song she ought to sing: Why am I always the bridesmaid, never the blushing bride. 'I'll ring you this afternoon to see if all the work's done!'

Aunt Elizabeth suddenly laughed. 'It's really absurd, but Nell and I will probably sit down again over another cup of tea and discuss the party!'

'There's lots of work to do!' Jo looked around her.

'Never mind. It's not every day one's only son gets engaged. Nell's wonderful for her age!'

'All right, then. I can see by the clock that I should have left a few minutes ago.'

''Bye, dear. I don't know what we'd do without you!'

'Oh, you'd manage!' Jo said softly, and allowed herself just the merest trace of bitterness. Aunt Elizabeth didn't hear her. She was going over the wedding plans in her mind. She fully intended that Jo should be one of the bridesmaids, but Jo had already decided to be well away by then. Saudi Arabia and find herself a rich sheik. There had to be some place she could find a little peace. Aunt Elizabeth was lovely, unfailingly kind to the lonely little girl Jo had been, but she saw nothing she didn't want to see and she had been protected from unpleasantness all her life. Now she was occupied most pleasurably in making plans for a big wedding. It would upset her to know Jo wouldn't be part of them, but Jo knew she wasn't brave enough or maybe foolish enough to fall in with these plans.

Uncle Joss was right: she would have to go on a trip. Someone had to be the loser. It was Blair's business. She would be out of a job that inspired her and filled her days meaningfully, but leaving Blair was the only way out. God knows she didn't want to. In her misery she had even considered staying and making a fight of it. How *could* he love her and marry someone else? If she stayed in the field she could still change his mind. She was even lunatic enough to dismiss his contemptuous

behaviour. The knowledge that he had been nervy and
upset lent weight to her chances. Were they right when
they said: All's fair in love and war? Julie could certainly afford a trip around the world. Jo had seen him
first. He had told her he loved her long before Julie had
moved in with her primrose curls. It was amusing and
perhaps not unusual the way in which her feelings were
see-sawing.

It was a beautiful day, clear and bright, plenty of
traffic on the road, but at least they had parking space at
the rear of the shop. She eased the little Datsun around
the corner and into the narrow street. This was an old
part of the city, recently trendy—an arts and crafts
centre with potters, painters, weavers, leather workers,
jewellery makers, contemporary furnishers and a hand-
ful of interior decorators and designers. Blair had most
beautifully restored the old terraced building they occupied, and it drew clients like a magnet. He really had
no need of Julie to be a great success. Experienced professionals admitted his scope and versatility.

Jo let herself in blessing the fact that it was Olive's
morning off. Not that she didn't like Olive, their Girl
Friday. She did. She was pert and amusing, though Blair
complained Olive didn't know her place, but she was
quick and reliable and Jo never had to tell her anything
twice. Olive, for her nineteen years, was also extremely
shrewd. It would have been hard indeed to fool her this
morning. The display rooms downstairs showed Blair's
sophisticated elegance to advantage—not that he
couldn't turn his hand to more forthright design. His
studio and sleeping pad was upstairs.

Immediately she got in, the phone rang. Jo went to it,
answering automatically: 'Leighton Interiors, Jo Adams
here!'

'Olive *here*, ducky!'

'Don't tell me, I can hear it. You've got a cold.'

'So what? I was out for a good time.'

'What's that supposed to mean?'

'Nothing, Jo. I wouldn't want to shock you. Listen, if you really need me, I'll come in. Martyr and all!' She produced a short, hoarse bark.

'No, you stay there. No need for us all to die.'

There was the muffled sound of a giggle and Jo inquired sharply: 'You're at home, aren't you, Olive?'

'Would you like to speak to me mum?'

'I wouldn't like to put you to the test. You *have* got a cold?'

'Would I lie to you?'

'Most people do!' Jo said before she could help herself.

'I *wouldn't*!' It came out as a whistling squeak, but the sincerity shone through.

'All right, dear. Ring me in the morning. Better ring Mum while you're at it!'

'Honestly, Jo, Mum's in the kitchen. Mr Leighton get away?'

'He'll be gone a week,' Jo told her.

'It says in the papers he's gone and got himself engaged to a strange lady.'

'Yes, Olive.'

'I can't feel he's doing the right thing. Neither does Mum. She really likes you.'

'It's not for any of us to say, Olive!'

'Gotcha! I'll be in in the morning. Don't forget I hold you in considerable respect.'

'Keep it up and I'll think I'm a doddering old lady!' laughed Jo.

Olive gave her sexy, breathy giggle. 'You're a dish. Andy thinks so!'

'Who's Andy? No, on second thoughts I don't want you to answer. There's the other phone. 'Bye, Olive!'

It turned out to be a call from Mrs Vaughn-Nugent, a jowly, wealthy lady who believed in keeping in daily contact. She didn't trouble to hide her disappointment

that Blair wasn't in, but actually she wanted to know
what he would fancy as an engagement present—
'Naughty boy!' Jo held her aching head, seeing herself
reflected in the mirrored wall, long legs and all. There
were a number of design briefs she had to go over. They
were constantly searching out new ideas, new colours,
new products, new materials. In the end Mrs Vaughn-
Nugent settled on something in sterling silver—'One
couldn't go wrong'—and threatened to ring back the
moment Blair arrived. If it was true, as Blair often
claimed, that she was very popular with the male clients,
the reverse was certainly true of him. Women fell for
him wholesale. They liked his elegant appearance and
his amber hooded eyes, the general air of culture about
him and the way he knew and appreciated beautiful
things. He was a brilliant and vastly ambitious man and
he knew how to use his very considerable charm. It was
all very sad and nerve-racking for her. She would be
treated now to an endless procession of calls following
the shock engagement announcement. At least Mrs
McConnell was still overseas. Being in a position of
wealth made things a lot easier.

Jo hung up her hat and ran a comb through her hair.
It fell in a heavy pageboy swing from a side parting. It
was sumptuous hair, worn in a simple style that never-
theless demanded expert cutting. The pure silk blouse
beneath the suit jacket was patterned in greens and she
wore a gold braid necklet and matching gold earrings
that ironically Blair had given her. He often saved her
time in this way, telling her where to go and buy her
clothes, his rapid and expert assessment almost woman
to woman. Or it had sometimes seemed that way.
Strange she should think of that now. Marsh McConnell,
for instance, might admire, but he would probably break
a leg getting out of a fashion boutique.

The first thing she had to do was ring Ed Harding, the
architect/designer and State President of the SIDA. She

would have to stand in for Blair at tomorrow night's meeting. Ed wouldn't mind. He was one of her greatest admirers—too fervent upon occasions. Jo went to pick up the phone, but a definite noise upstairs startled her out of all proportion. When her heart stopped its loud thumping she considered it would be Cleo, the shop cat. But surely Blair would have left her out. Cleo was generally petted and fed all along the street, slept at the potter's, but she was most faithful in her fashion to Blair. Then again it could be an intruder. There were a few valuable antiques from Blair's private collection upstairs. She picked up a heavy ashtray and walked towards the stairs, half convinced it was Cleo.

A man was coming down them and the ashtray fell out of her nerveless hand and harmlessly on to the carpet.

'Blair!' she exclaimed.

'You didn't think I was going away without talking to you?'

'What about your early morning appointment at Begg's?'

'I've already cancelled that. I'll catch up on them tomorrow!'

He was staring at her hypnotically and for the space of a few seconds Jo felt completely defeated. 'It's true what your father says, isn't it? It *must* be. You use people!'

'When did Dad say that?' he asked, as if it were a compliment, not a cruelty.

'Does it matter!' Her heart was beating loudly in the stillness. 'Look, Blair, I have nothing to say to you, unless somehow you've changed your mind!'

'I'm a designer, not an acrobat!' he said wryly, and he actually smiled.

'And you fully intend going ahead with your plan to marry Julie?'

'You make it sound like a military operation, pet!'

'Put it down to my state of shock.'

'It will pass,' he said smoothly.

'I think not!' With a swift movement she put a table between them. 'You've got a frightening tendency to ignore other people's pain. It's really odd, do you know that?'

He was by no means discouraged, coming towards her with the stamp of elegance on him. 'I want you on my side, Jo!' he said in a low, moving voice.

'I'm not surprised!' She held up a hand as if to restrain him. 'You want it all ways.'

He came round the edge of the table and they were face to face now. She could see the muscle pulling in his lightly tanned cheek. He didn't look well seen up close, nerve-ridden, with a slight puffiness beneath his hooded amber eyes. Her heart smote her and she wondered if she was doomed to love him no matter how badly he damaged her. The familiar compassion she felt was showing in her own eyes and Blair put out a hand like a charmer to caress the satiny skin at the side of her neck while her dark hair fell over his sleeve.

'Jo!'

The memory of their lovemaking clung to her like a second skin, and her traitorous flesh was stirring. She couldn't answer, the colour drained from her face. Her heavy lashes fell over her eyes and she broke away from him in an effort at final renunciation. 'Don't touch me!'

'You make me out a brute, heartless! You know I'm not!'

'*Please*, Blair!' her voice implored him. 'What devil drives you? I know you're unhappy!'

'I am!' he assured her.

'Then how can you go through with this?' The words left her lips, rising with anger.

'Let's say my ambitions are greater than my love for you!'

She gasped with the pain and turned her back on him. 'Is that what you stayed behind to say?'

'The devil I did!' he said fiercely. 'I just want to be sure you're here when I get back!'

The urgent clamour of the phone distracted them, and Jo gestured towards it almost wildly. 'Aren't you going to answer that?'

'No!' His tone was sufficient to make her pick up the phone from long habit.

'Leighton Interiors!' she said, crushing down an up-rush of hysteria.

'Oh, good, you're in!' Aunt Elizabeth said brightly.

In a state of perturbation Jo swung about. She couldn't find it in her heart to tell Blair's mother he was standing right behind her, one hand at her waist. 'Anything wrong?' she asked, clutching the phone.

'The reverse!' Aunt Elizabeth carolled excitedly. 'Guess who just rang? Mr McConnell!' she swept on without waiting for an answer. 'He called to thank me for giving such a beautiful party. My, he has got a sexy voice on the phone. A woman could bloom with a voice like that around!'

'Yes, dear?' Jo prompted. 'Has this anything to do with anything?'

'Of course!' The lightish voice dropped a few decibels. 'He asked for you and I had to tell him you were going in to the shop. Just thought I'd warn you, because he said he'd be popping in. I told him where it was!'

'I thought you were on my side?' Jo cried, her body automatically tensing for flight.

'I *am* on your side. That's why I sent him.'

'You mean he's on his way now?'

Jo could hear the shrug. 'Well, not exactly. I really don't know. He didn't mention time.'

'Maybe I'd better lock up as soon as I hear footsteps!' said Jo dryly.

'You and your wisecracks! Take my advice, go out to lunch—somewhere madly expensive. I don't think it would hurt!'

'What would Blair say?' she said, sharper than she should.

'Blair's future is settled. Now it's your turn. I know the normal female reaction to Mr McConnell. I'm not that old!'

'Funny,' said Jo, 'he infuriates me!'

'I don't believe you!' Aunt Elizabeth laughed gaily. 'You know what they say, there's a thin line between love and hate!'

'I certainly am glad to hear that,' smiled Jo. 'Listen, dear, I'll have to go. It promises to be a busy morning!'

Aunt Elizabeth rang off with a 'Take my advice!' and Jo replaced the receiver, keeping her hand on it.

'Mother?' Blair asked, having heard her voice. 'What did she want?'

'She was warning me that Marsh McConnell intends calling in.'

Anger darkened Blair's face. 'Doesn't he know you work here?'

'That's what I'm trying to do, if you'd only go away.'

'Will you be here when I get back?' He caught her shoulders and turned her around, his eyes narrowed and fixed hard on her.

'I'd better make it plain now. I'm leaving you, Blair. I'm surprised I have to give you an explanation.'

He looked deeply into her eyes and she had a sensation of giddiness and panic. 'Your feelings are too strong for you to leave me. You couldn't go on without me!'

'Yes, Blair, that's what you'd like to believe!'

The phone rang again and he threw out a hand in savage irritation. 'Leave it!'

'What *is* this?' she asked jaggedly. 'You can't tempt me with anything. Go away, Blair. Just go away!'

'You're afraid of losing your control, aren't you?'

It was unmistakably the truth. She was slumped back against a cabinet, upset beyond endurance, a hundred mixed emotions flashing across her face. It was time to press his advantage. 'You *can't* leave me!' he said in a low, vibrant undertone. 'It will be never before feeling is dead between us!'

She continued to look down blindly and he swept her towards him, holding her resisting body close to his own. 'This marriage of mine, what does it mean? Plenty of women marry for security, why not a man? It won't affect us. Look at me, Jo!'

'I want you to go away!' she said tightly, feeling the same terrible fascination.

'And I'm not going until you tell me you love me!'

His handsome face seemed to blur in a red mist of rage. 'Don't talk to me about love!' she hurled at him. 'You're mad and ruthless and I won't fall in with your plans, not if my life depended upon it!'

The colour had flared into her cheeks and her eyes were sparkling like emeralds. She looked so wild and beautiful Blair bent his head with a muffled groan, searching for her mouth with a desperation that was hard to evade. 'I want you, Jo. Just for this minute, to hell with everyone else!'

She struggled violently, but her heated senses were flaming through her body.

'Witch, little witch!'

Jo went limp and he began to kiss her deeply, trying to revive the passion that had burned so brightly between them. Her slender body was shuddering in his arms so that everything was going out of range, inciting him, her mouth crushed under his own. 'Jo darling, you belong to me. Let me love you, properly. Please, darling!'

She was lost ... lost ... sinking into a sensual oblivion where nothing mattered and all seemed permissible, consumed again by her love for him. His hands were moving under the jacket of her suit, heating the silk, cupping her vulnerable breasts. Possessive hands that thought now at last he could take her.

On the brink of surrender pride spurted to save her,

then conscience to further upbraid her. She tried to arch away from him, her flesh and her brain committed to rejecting him, when he was literally torn from her arms and sent reeling across the room, his slim frame crashing into a high-backed Italian chair. He staggered and fell with a groan and Jo, after one distraught glance at his assailant, hastened to help him.

'Splendid!' Marsh McConnell said harshly, an intolerable menace in his powerful frame. 'Why don't you two spend your worthless passion? Or have you already, in this cosy little set-up?' The black eyes burned.

As Blair tried to get up the colour seeped right away from under his skin, his slightness of build was all the more pronounced. 'Don't jump to any hasty conclusions, McConnell, and don't blame Jo!'

'*Blair!*' Jo whispered, her eyes on his face.

'Stand away from him!' McConnell ordered with deadly quiet.

'How did you get in here?' Shaken, Jo got to her feet. His dark head was bent forward, muscles coiled and she had the sickening impression of a panther about to spring. They confronted one another like adversaries, the contempt in his eyes lashing her.

'What fools you are!' he said with shocking enmity. 'Both of you too ... *satiated* to hear someone coming. It could have been anyone, a client, competitor—or are they used to this kind of thing?'

Jo's green eyes didn't leave him, as though holding him with her gaze she lessened the danger. 'You can't take everything from me, so don't try!'

'I haven't even started on you!' he said, and she suddenly knew what Uncle Joss had meant about crossing him. 'What about lover-boy here, shouldn't he be hundreds of miles away?'

Blair had risen and was standing quite still, his whitened face the very picture of despair. 'Just a minute, McConnell,' he said quietly.

The bigger man swung on him. 'What kind of a man are you anyway?'

'Can I help it if Jo's in love with me?'

'You swine!' He looked as if it would give him great pleasure to smash Blair's smooth face in.

Jo ran in front of him, her hands flung out sideways in a gesture of pleading. 'Humiliate *me*. Go on, that's what you mean to do!'

'And you love this miserable cur?' Marsh asked her harshly. 'Do women love men who treat them so vilely? Damn you for the little fool you are!'

'I couldn't help it!' she said, taking the full blame on herself. It was obvious that not even this could change Blair's plans. 'Haven't you ever loved anyone?' she asked the man who stared at her with such contemptuous intensity.

'I'd let no woman make a fool of me.'

'*Please*, Jo!' Blair begged in a suffering voice.

'Shut up!' said Marsh McConnell as if he had a powerful urge towards violence.

'What are you going to do?' Jo asked gravely. 'Take away Julie's faith in him?'

'Do you think it would give me pleasure? She loves him.'

'More than that!' Blair said swiftly. 'I love her!'

'But you can't renounce the desire you feel for another woman? And don't tell me you don't want her. That's entirely too rich. I saw the way you were holding her.'

'Jo and I intend to split up!' Blair said briefly.

'And I'll be just the one to see you do. Don't think for one moment I approve Julie's choice of a husband. In fact I haven't decided yet what I'm going to do. Julie has to be protected from herself.'

Blair's amber eyes under their heavy lids were brightening. 'Anything you have to say against me would only drive Julie further into my arms.'

'She can cut her losses as well as the next woman!'

'Like Jo?' Blair asked cruelly.

Marsh McConnell's right hand clenched in a way Jo found unnerving. She almost threw herself at him, and he looked down at her with his brilliant black eyes. 'I could ruin Leighton,' he told her.

'It might rebound on you. You said Julie's happiness is all-important. It's useless for you to deny the extent of her love for him. He *wants* to marry her. Can't you see that?'

'Can you?' he asked curtly.

'Blair's right!' she said, only then realising her hand was clasped around his wrist. 'There's nothing between us. Not ever again.'

'No doubt we can arrange to lock you up!'

'You're being unfair to Jo!' Blair protested, his fair hair fallen forward in a golden wave.

Marsh raised his hand briefly. 'I suggest you shut up.'

Jo caught her breath expecting a fight, but Blair was clearly stepping out of the arena. Humiliation could be borne, but not the loss of Julie's fortune. Her knees nearly buckled under her and Marsh pushed her into a chair.

'I have to think this thing over. I may be serving Julie better by telling her what I've just seen.'

Jo could see the fright in Blair's eyes and she ran her tongue over her dry mouth. 'I told you, I'll be the one to go.'

'Isn't that touching? You're going to sacrifice yourself for the man you love but can't marry.' He looked down at her lovely face and smiled with grimness. 'Why don't you hate him?'

'That's impossible!' she whispered with very real emotion. 'We've been together too long.'

'Now it's my affair. You're not staying here another day longer.' He turned and glanced at Blair, a man of towering self-assurance and superb strength. The glittering black eyes narrowed over Blair's smooth, handsome face, his beautifully tailored suit, the slim compact body. 'Time's money, isn't it, Leighton? Shouldn't you be some place else?'

'I can't go away not knowing what's happening here.'

'Too bad. Hang a sign on the door.'

The phone rang again and Marsh picked it up, his voice deep and meticulously controlled. In astonishment Jo heard him say Mr Leighton was interstate and the shop would be shut for a week. The caller persisted and he then said Miss Adams had a virus, making it appear she was very much in bed and not right beside him.

'Well, well!' Jo exclaimed, 'if another war breaks out I'm sure you'll make General. Aren't you going to protest, Blair, or are you just going to stand there and let him run your business as well.'

'Circumstances alter everything, Jo!' Blair agonised. 'What else can we do? I must meet my appointments, and McConnell here has the whip hand.'

'And doesn't he love to use it?' Jo said bitterly.

'It hasn't touched you yet, lady!'

Jo shrugged and looked up at him, not without humour. 'After today, Marsh McConnell, you're not the man who's going to give *me* orders!'

'I think you're destined for a magnificent setdown!'

Blair was listening sharply, becoming once more the elegant designer. 'You're a man of the world, McConnell. These things happen. It would be best for all of us to put it right out of our minds.'

Marsh McConnell smiled and something in his face made Blair flush scarlet. 'You've reason to be afraid of me, Leighton.'

'I want peace!' Blair said briefly. 'Let's not play games. What happened here this morning will never happen again. I think you know that, McConnell.'

'Oh, I'm sure of it!' the other man responded with a dark kind of amusement. 'My mother was highly impressed by you, but frankly, I think you're a greedy man.'

'What's going to happen to Jo?' Blair asked belatedly.

'You leave her to me.'

Jo got up with a little flourish and began to collect her things. Nothing could threaten her now. She'd lost Blair, lost her job. Nothing was sad, so why did she feel as though her balance was gone? 'If you've really nothing else to say to me, General, I'll go!'

'Leighton's the one who's going. Aren't you, Leighton? We'll shut up here, and I want you to know you're not in the clear!'

Blair was furiously angry, but he was holding it down. A few hasty words could ruin his future. Towards Marsh McConnell he felt a bitter hostility, but he was dependent on the man's silence. Jo he knew to the core. She would never strike him down; revenge wasn't her way. 'I've my briefcase to collect!' he announced into the brilliant silence.

'Go and get it. I'll ring you a cab!' Marsh McConnell said coolly.

Blair didn't appear grateful. 'Don't bother. There's a stand at the corner.'

After he had moved away from them Marsh McConnell inquired laconically, 'What's upstairs?'

'Blair's studio,' Jo answered, the cold finger of premonition on her neck.

'No doubt he sleeps there occasionally.'

'Not with me. That's what you're trying to say.'

'And where do you live, Miss Adams?'

'None of your business!' she said shortly.

'Don't you want a lift home?'

'I've got the Datsun outside.'

'Where do you manage to put your long legs?' he demanded.

'Not all of us are immensely rich, Mr McConnell.'

'You're very haughty, aren't you, for a two-timing

woman?' he drawled, as dark as a gypsy and just as bold.

'How can a pirate like you act the prude?' demanded Jo crossly.

'Funny you should say that! I've the very definite intention of making off with you.'

Blair, descending the stairs, was a party to these words. A black jealousy filled his heart, but caution was there. He could wait. 'I'd be grateful if you could make one or two calls for me, Jo, seeing the shop will be shut.'

'Really, Blair, I've given of my level best.'

'I think so too!' Marsh McConnell offered sardonically. 'All she *can* do is put up the sign!'

'It's my fault, I admit it!' Blair said generously. 'I should have had it out with Jo long ago. The last thing I've ever wanted to do is hurt her. Jo and I played together as children.'

'Ah well, averaging it out you've had more than enough of her time. So long, Leighton!' Marsh McConnell came away from leaning on the table, a big man from whom it was no use to look for pity or pardon.

Jo didn't even glance in Blair's direction. Perhaps she was going mad, but the sight of him was hurting her unbearably. Didn't a man fight and with any sort of luck, win? Blair on his talents alone would go far. Did he really have to swallow the bitter pill of Marsh McConnell's domination?

The door closed on Blair and remained closed. 'We don't seem to have a sign to cover the occasion!' she said, and of all things burst into tears.

'Poor suffering child!' he grinned in black amusement.

'You brute!'

'Ah, Josephine, I'm trying to take care of you.'

'For God's sake, why?' she demanded.

'I'm not saying. There are a lot of flaws in you. It's

just dawned on me Leighton will do a lot better with Julie!'

'And you're going to make sure I stay away?'

'Dry your eyes,' he ordered. 'You look like a drowned mermaid, if there is such a thing!'

'I'm disgusted. Absolutely disgusted.'

'It's your own fault and no use crying about it. Here, get me a bit of cardboard.'

'I might as well.' Jo swallowed on the tears in her throat and searched out a suitable piece. 'It's nice to know someone around here is enjoying himself!'

Marsh went and sat down at the table and pulled the cardboard towards him, producing a gold pen from his pocket and writing in a bold sweeping hand. 'That does it, I guess!'

'What did you say?' She turned away from the mirror and the study of her pale face.

'All I can say. Closed until the 22nd. Now, to find some prominent place!'

'Try the window. There really are a few things I should take care of.'

He came back from the window and began to walk towards her. 'I want you to promise me something, Josephine. Stay away from Leighton.'

'You do realise that his family are my family?'

'Then why don't they know about you.'

'Uncle Joss does. Aunt Elizabeth would never guess.'

'You mean she doesn't want to,' he corrected. 'She's a very charming little lady, but she would avoid unpleasantness like the plague.'

'I have a fearful headache!' she said aimlessly, and put a trembling hand to her temple.

'I have to see some friends of mine,' Marsh told her. 'Come with me.'

'I'm sorry, *no*!'

'Think again!'

'You're not going to blackmail me as well?'

'You got the idea first,' he drawled.

'I'm too bewildered to make good company.'

'After what I've seen this morning I begin to ask myself whether I should keep you permanently in sight! You've the makings of a very bad girl!'

'*You* choose to think that!' said Jo, annoyed by his tone.

'You'll have to persuade me you're not!'

'You sound as if you expect me to dedicate my life to it!'

He opened the door and stood there waiting for her; 'Don't be nervous!'

'I'm never nervous!' she said, swallowing visibly.

'Now there's a statement I can't accept!'

Jo swung back abruptly for a last look at the special environment she had thought of as an expression of their lives: hers and Blair's. Making Leighton Interiors highly successful had been one of her goals; marrying Blair had been another. He had had a great influence on her. Now she had to give him up. The whole thing went deeply, but all life was an attempt to cover up. She gave a faint sigh, feeling quite isolated from the life she had known.

'Don't go carrying any burning torches!' Marsh McConnell said with more than a hint of steel. 'I take good care of my own!'

'Lucky Julie!' She looked back in time to catch his expression of scorn. It suited him. Probably if she liked the type she would have called him a very handsome man, with dark flaunting good looks and a great impression of vigour. In her mind's eye she could see Blair's golden grace and her heart gave a nervous start.

'Come along, Josephine!' Marsh shrugged his wide shoulders. 'What will be, *will* be!'

'Who's making a fuss?' she said, in a tired, defeated voice.

'That's what you say now! Actually you'll recover

and probably be a very happy woman as well!' He took her arm and she fell silent, knowing it was useless to try and beat a retreat. She had never felt less like going visiting, but right at that moment she had neither the strength nor the will to oppose him. He would just fling her over his shoulder anyway. She didn't have the slightest doubt he had some notorious ancestor in the background anyway. Guardedly she looked up into his face and found it speculative and mocking and essentially distrustful of any woman with green eyes.

'Let's go, Miss Adams,' he said coolly. 'Who knows, you might be embarking on a new career!'

CHAPTER THREE

THE Symons lived in the western suburbs on a beautiful three-acre property that backed on to the wide, deep river. It was a near-perfect physical location, the house obscured from the road by towering gums and a prolific spring array of shrubbery that flowered right down the red-gravelled drive: the kind of property that spelled money, and Jo didn't relish intruding, being a great respector of privacy.

'Why so silent?' Marsh demanded.

'I'm wondering why you invited me.'

'Anne will be glad of your company. It might even be good therapy for both of you. Anne hasn't had much to smile about lately—she lost a baby just under a year ago.'

'Oh, I *am* sorry!' Jo said fervently, echoing all women's pain.

'They have two others,' he said gravely. 'Paddy and Jenny, six and eight—delightful kids. Dave and I were at university together and we've always kept in touch. They've been out to the property and I always visit them here. I was their best man, as a matter of fact, and I expect Dave will be mine!'

'Exit one very eligible bachelor!' she said dryly.

'I haven't been caught yet!' His black eyes challenged her. 'Anyway, to fill you in before we get there, Anne has been suffering from an acute depression and I know Dave's worried.'

'It would be very hard to recover from a tragedy like that,' she said soberly. 'These things are to be accepted, but it's so very hard!'

'She *must* put it in the past, for her own sake,' said

Marsh. 'Life can be cruel, but she still has Dave and the other children.'

'It's strange, isn't it,' she mused, 'how we all call a halt on one another? One is only allowed a certain time to grieve, then one must close a door on it.'

'We have to bring Anne back to us,' he said grimly.

'Are you sure she'll want to see me?'

'You might offer a solution!'

'I'm not with you.'

'No time to explain. Anne has been badly hurt. You may find her a little quiet and withdrawn. Dave and the kids are just the same.' Marsh slid the car in under an enormous flowering jacaranda that drew the eye in its radiance and Jo turned her head to look at the house.

'If it's as good on the inside as it is from the outside, it would be lovely to decorate!'

'I thought you were going to give all that away?' Marsh queried.

'How can I? I work for a living, Mr McConnell.'

He came around to her side and helped her out. 'Save a word and make it *Marsh*!'

'I think I prefer James!'

'That would only make it confusing. Even my mother calls me Marsh. Get set, here's the kids. Plus the dogs. I hope you like Afghans. They like a lot of space!'

Flying across the grass in beautiful, joyful abandon were two magnificent silver thoroughbreds, ringed tails held high, their long silky coats flying in the wind of their own springy motion. Two children were running very fast after them with no hope of catching them.

'The kids have had a day off school in my honour,' Marsh explained. 'Dave works at home these days. He's an architect, but he pulled out of his partnership. Anne needed him. Hey there!' The dogs were upon them and so they wouldn't knock her down, Marsh stood in front of Jo, taking the full brunt of their affectionate welcome. 'Meet Judah and Augusta. They're natural show-offs!'

'That's nothing! Aunt Elizabeth had a poodle that used to play the piano!' she countered.

'You're kidding!'

'No, it's true. It was even thinking of taking singing lessons.'

'You could have made a lot of money with that. Here, don't be shy, Judah wants to shake your hand.'

'Who's shy?' Jo took the extended paw and shook it. 'How do you do, Judah. Any more tricks up your sleeve?'

'Only one, dancing on your shoulders—but you'd better leave that one. We wouldn't want to mark that suit!'

'As a matter of fact I think it's going to be!' Jo turned her head to catch up with the children's progress. 'The little fellow is about to skid on the wet grass!'

Marsh, still controlling the Afghan invasion, looked up in time to see one small flying figure measure its length on the grass some little distance from the whirling jet of the sprinkler. In another second Jo was beside it, dropping down to her knees.

'Hi, I'm Jo!'

Blue eyes blinked in an embarrassed little face.

'Uncle Marsh's girl-friend?'

'Not precisely!' Jo helped him to his feet while he steadied himself against her and seeing he had no objection she began to brush him down. 'That was nearly a bad fall!'

'Thank you.'

'You're welcome. You must be Patrick?'

'Paddy mostly. Nanna and Pop call me Patrick. We've been waiting and waiting for you to arrive!' He looked up at her with his entrancing wide smile and for the first time saw the marks of his wet, grassy hands on the jacket of her suit. 'Oh, look what I've done!' he exclaimed, his face instantly crumpling.

'As a matter of fact it's rather good!' Jo looked down

at her suit in amazement. 'There's a perfect set of prints!'

'We're not allowed to watch the F.B.I.!' Paddy said virtuously.

'No hard feelings!' Jo clutched his hand in her own and it curled up confidingly.

'Do you have dogs at home?' he asked.

'Only a cat. I couldn't have two Afghans in an apartment.'

'What's that?'

'It's a place one has to adjust to when one doesn't have a home of one's own. You know, a block of flats!'

'I bet it follows you around,' observed Paddy.

'What?'

'The cat. Here comes Jenny and Dad. Don't take any notice of Jenny. She's been waiting just as long as I have!'

A tall man who just had to be Paddy's father came towards her, a rueful, apologetic smile on his face. 'That was some welcome! I'll understand your feelings if you want to rage!'

'Why should I? It won me a friend!'

Marsh introduced them and Jo put out her hand. 'It's very nice of you to have me, Mr Symons.'

'*Dave*, please!' His very blue eyes sparkled over her, then he turned to his friend. 'Couldn't you have protected this beautiful lady?'

'I've been trying to do that since I first laid eyes on her!'

'Meet Jenny!' said Jenny's father, pushing her forward.

Jenny smiled up at her with just a shade of feminine reserve, a distinctive, intelligent-looking little girl with fair plaits and grey eyes. 'You were unlucky to meet Paddy first!' she observed. 'Anyone who lives with him knows he's accident-prone!'

'And you had no business turning on the sprinkler!'

Paddy said wrathfully. 'I've been careful all morning!'

'That will do!' their father said firmly. 'Consider we have guests!'

'Yes, and it's wonderful!' Paddy went back to his expansive, all-embracing smile. He was still holding Jo's hand and all together they began to walk back towards the house. Marsh glanced across at Jo with a smiling mockery, obviously seeing some significance in the way she had gained Paddy's instant allegiance. No male was too small, his black eyes seemed to say. For that very reason it was senseless to let her get out of sight. She drew ahead with Paddy, who began to chatter away about being off school, and the two men fell into conversation, Jenny having arranged herself between them in the particular way of the sexes, holding each by the hand.

'Here comes Mummy!' said Paddy. 'She's very sad mostly!'

'Oh, I am sorry!' Jo sympathised.

'Do you like babies?'

'Oh yes!'

'We lost ours,' the child said sadly.

Jo couldn't answer, but she pressed his hand consolingly. Anne Symons was coming down the short flight of steps to meet them, another petite blonde, but with an important difference. Tragedy lay on her like a grey veil. It marked her fair skin and drew lustre from her hair and her grey eyes. A faint colour came to her skin as Marsh went towards her, resting his hands on her shoulders, then dropping a kiss on her fragile, upturned brow. Whether she wanted to withdraw or not he was bringing her forward to meet Jo, and the moment was filled with remonstrations as Anne saw the havoc Paddy's grubby hands had wrought on Jo's beautiful white jacket.

It actually took a little bit of time calming her, and somehow Jo found herself acting the older, stronger, more capable sister rather than a complete stranger some several years younger than her highly strung hostess. She dismissed the whole thing lightly, not in the least perturbed about a few marks on her jacket. Anne led her through to the main bedroom where she could put down her things and freshen up in the adjoining en suite bathroom.

'Marsh tells me you're an interior designer?' she called.

Jo walked back into the bedroom minus her jacket which she had left hanging up in the bathroom, the worst of the grass stains sponged off. 'Yes, I'm with Leighton Interior,' she said lightly, her green eyes moving over Anne's rather fey, pale face.

'What a beautiful blouse!' exclaimed Anne. 'It goes exactly with the colour of your eyes. I'm sure David knows your boss. Blair Leighton, isn't it?'

'Yes.'

'How remarkable that he should be marrying Julie!'

'Yes, it's a small world, as they say,' Jo agreed.

'Don't let David talk shop over lunch!' Anne warned, and a fugitive smile came to her face. She was actually a little healed by Jo's outgoing and basically managing nature and her expression registered her very real admiration. 'I know he recommends different designers from time to time to his clients. He's one of the new breed, determined to see the interior match up with the exterior design.'

'And he's obviously very talented!' Jo's eyes swept around the muted luxury of the room.

'Yes!' Anne agreed, and a shutter came over her eyes.

In the little silence Jo stood there catching some of Anne's distressed state of mind. Anne looked up, saw her expression and flushed. 'Don't mind me, Jo. I've grown very introspective. I suppose it shows?'

'Don't feel guilty about it!' Jo leaned forward and touched her hand.

'What I really want,' said Anne in an agonised rush, 'is my baby son!'

She looked like a small broken bird, perched so warily on the bed, and Jo dropped down beside her, moved to call her back from the brink of despair. 'Nothing so terrible has ever happened to me, Anne, so I don't know how I would react myself, but please don't let your grief crush you. I'm certain no one could have a more loving little family than you've got!'

'Yes!' Anne whispered, her hands folded tightly in her lap. 'I used to be quite different, you know.'

'I like you the way you are!' Jo assured her.

'No, it's true. I don't even pay much attention to my appearance any more. You've made me think of that—so glossy and beautiful. Losing Jamie—we named him after Marsh—turned me into another woman. I know I'm denying David the girl he fell in love with. I don't play with the children any more or even really listen to all they tell me. It's almost like turning into another human being.'

'Have you had a change of scene since it happened?'

'No, no!' Anne continued to wring her hands. 'I haven't wanted to go away. More than anything I cling to the children I've got. Jamie's was a cot death. He was a beautiful, healthy baby in the night and dead the next morning. A mother should learn to accept these things, but I can't. I keep thinking why did it happen? Where did I go wrong?'

'Please, Anne!' begged Jo.

Anne sighed. 'I have to stop, haven't I?'

'For your own sake. Grief is a citadel and we're really the only ones who can let ourselves out. You still have lots of love in your life.'

'Haven't you?' Anne glanced up, looking calmer.

'Why do you ask?'

'You spoke so strangely.'

'I haven't got what you've got, Anne—a husband who

loves me and two lovely healthy children.'

Anne seemed to hold her breath. 'Do you live alone, Jo?'

'Yes. My mother left my father when I was about Jenny's age. My father never forgave her or me. He died a few years ago.'

'Oh, I am sorry!' Anne sat and stared at her, her eyes taking in every detail of Jo's face. 'My childhood was such a happy one. But a beautiful girl like you would have more admirers than you could possibly cope with.'

'The one I wanted got away!' Jo said wryly.

'Then of course you know the pain of loss,' Anne murmured quietly.

'It would be nothing compared to yours.'

Anne continued to stare at her for a few seconds, then she patted her hand. 'I'm a fool, Jo. Someone has hurt you cruelly. I can see it at the back of your eyes. You're not just a good listener, you really *know*!'

'The trouble is, what to do next. One can't remain in prison. Life moves on.'

'I'm very grateful to you for saying that,' said Anne. 'David has tried to tell me over and over, but somehow I haven't listened. I've allowed my grief to spread to my family, and David has been so good. Men aren't allowed to cry. There's always a family to support.'

'But it's worth it!'

'Yes, it is!' Anne stood up and smiled. 'Let's have a cup of tea. When did you meet Marsh?'

'Only last night.'

Anne looked towards the mirror and adjusted her short curls. 'He's absolutely first rate. We all adore him. He was our best man. Marsh was the star turn in their university days and David was always the runner-up. They took different courses, of course, but they always met on the field. Now Marsh controls a splendid chain of properties. You should get him to take you out to Malakai,' she went on. 'It means secret place and it's the wildest, most beautiful place on earth. The children only saw it the once, but they decided it was just about the place they wanted to spend the rest of their lives. Do you know the Outback well?'

'I regret to say I don't know it at all,' Jo confessed.

'We'll get Marsh to change that. Malakai is the farthest west. The landscape is unbelievable—the quality of *light*, the pottery colours, so burnt yet so vigorous! It makes the blood rush to the head. It's truly the home of the Dreamtime gods. One can almost feel they still walk there. Marsh exactly fits his environment. One glance is enough to tell he's totally out of the ordinary.'

'Yes, he does create a certain image!' Jo tried hard to sound enthusiastic. Evidently it fooled Anne, who unexpectedly gave an impish smile.

'Get him to invite you to Malakai!'

'He did make a promise of sorts,' Jo admitted.

'Well then...!' Smiling, Jo could see that Anne restored to her old bloom would be a very attractive woman with a subtle, understated beauty, her large, well spaced grey eyes her most charming feature. 'I'm so glad you came, Jo,' she said softly.

'So am I!' Green eyes smiled into grey. 'Perhaps it was written.'

'I feel like that too!'

'Tell me, did you do all your own interior design?' Jo asked.

'I had David to inspire my imagination!'

Together they went out to rejoin the others, conscious that some strong bond had been forged between them. After that, the time seemed to fly and Dave was seen to look frequently at his wife, pathetically grateful for such increasing flashes of her former animation. In such glorious weather it had been decided to have lunch on the patio looking down towards the river where a beautiful white-faced heron searched the shallows for food. The children had already provided salad offerings from their own surprisingly luxuriant vegetable patch, and there was pink, juicy ham and roast chicken, freshly baked croissants and an excellent Riesling chilled to perfection. Jo looked down at their shining heads with a strange kind of pain. They were delightful children, intelligent and friendly, and they too were conscious that something had put their mother in a tranquil humour.

Against her will she was drawn to look at Marsh McConnell. The last thing she expected was to find him observing *her*, his sculptured, very definite mouth faintly twisted. Every time she looked at him his face seemed to alter. It was a mobile face, a disquietening face in its strength and enormous vitality, and somehow it seemed to her barbaric! All he needed was gold earrings and the wind through those raven curls. Her eyes seemed riveted to him and she put it down to the sun on her head and two glasses of wine. Images of Blair unlocked beneath her eyes, but they were wavery, like a face under water. There was only one face she could see, Marsh McConnell's, and a feeling of fatalism settled around her. She would have to do whatever he wanted, and there was a suggestion of it in his face. Blair too would be dependent on what he decided. Blair, who couldn't forgo a woman's inheritance. She would have to put it out of her mind.

Dave went to refill her glass and she smiled at him with all the unconscious allure of a siren. 'Dave, *please*, all I'll want to do is sleep and sleep!'

'Why not down there among the flowers!' Marsh broke in dryly. 'Don't give her another one, Dave!'

'She seems all right to me,' said Dave.

'It's not the proper time. I've got something I've saved up to say.'

'Then give it to us, pal.'

'Can you give us a clue?' Anne too was looking dreamy and Marsh met her smiling eyes.

'This is something you must do if you want to please me.'

'Anything!' She reached over and touched his hand, always at ease with him.

The children, sitting on either side of him, were tingling with excitement. 'Tell us, Uncle Marsh!'

'All right, then. How would you two like a long holiday on Malakai?'

'Oh, beaut!' Their faces were moving pictures and their exclamations led to a general free-for-all where they hopped up from their chairs, unable to contain their excitement, Paddy launching himself at Marsh like a missile, associating him in his mind with wonderful things like horses and cattle and the great open spaces; flying through the air in one's own plane; mustering stock from a helicopter.

'Now, Paddy!' his mother scolded gently, and took hold of him. 'You sound as if you mean it, Marsh?'

'Of course I do. Just as much I intend you two, you and Dave, to take a holiday together. It's high time you did, and you will, if you still want to stay my friend!'

'I can't, Marsh!' she said in a heartbreaking voice.

Dave was looking very hard at his hands, long-fingered and clever. Marsh had said something of this to him earlier and though he longed to get Anne away he was prepared to hear her reject Marsh's merciful suggestion out of hand. He had carefully kept his own grief from her, but he knew he couldn't produce his best work until Anne settled and accepted their tragedy.

Jo noted the bewildered emotions on Anne's face, but she said nothing. A brilliant copper light was filtering through the vine-wreathed pergola catching all the gold lights in Anne's hair. Her expression was back to that of haunting sadness, but Marsh clearly intended to shock her out of it.

'You're too exhausted, Anne, to make the decision. Dave, how about it?'

'I'm thirty-four,' Dave confessed, 'and I haven't seen the States!'

'Then I don't understand you at all! There are planes flying over there every day.'

Surprisingly Anne found her voice. 'But you're much too busy, Marsh, to look after the children, and Mrs Hays has more than enough on her hands.'

Marsh held up his hand in a gesture of authority, his eyes sparkling like jets between their thick curling lashes. 'Some things are ordained!' he said almost tenderly. 'We have with us today Josephine, who is looking for a temporary position!'

'But Jo has a job!' Anne protested.

'No, she's going to start up a little business of her own. All hush-hush, of course. Quite a few people have been trying to get hold of her and Leighton would be the last person to clip her wings. They grew up together. Right, Jo?'

'I'm slow!' said Jo.

'*He* isn't!' Dave choked back a laugh.

'Before Jo enslaves herself in her hothouse world again,' Marsh continued, 'I think she should see a little of nature's beauty. The seasons have been prodigal lately. Malakai will dazzle you. If you'll come with me and help look after the children I can promise you a whole new world!'

Paddy chose that very minute to break away from his mother and encircle Jo's neck in an altogether pleading grip.

'Would you, Jo? Nothing will happen if you won't!'

'Well—' Jo gazed into Paddy's sunny little face for a minute, 'if Mummy and Daddy are content to leave you in my care, I'll promise to look after you as if you were my very own.'

Anne gave a little gulping sob and thrust back her chair. Her face worked for a moment, but she couldn't get anything out. Dave stood up instantly, peering very anxiously into her face.

'Anne darling!'

Anne gave in to the strange panic within her. She turned about and ran through the house.

'Go after her!' Marsh said briskly.

'She mightn't want me!'

'Hell, man!' Marsh stared at his friend, and after a tormented second Dave too went back through the house, where no door had slammed.

Jo turned to the children who stood there wide-eyed. 'Mummy is just a little upset. She doesn't want to leave you, you see.'

'Gee, we'll be good!' Paddy assured her.

'It's not that!' Jenny answered him shrilly. 'You just had to mess everything up falling over this morning, and she can't decide if it's safe to leave you.'

'No, it's not that!' said Marsh very definitely. 'You'd really like to come?'

'Oh, we'd *love* to!' both children chorused excitedly.

'Then show me you can follow a direction. Go and play for a while until the matter is decided.'

'May we have an apple?' they asked.

'Yes, of course!' Jo picked up two shiny Jonathans and passed them over.

'Come with us, Jo?' Jenny asked, full of consideration. 'We could play table tennis.'

'Jo's going to stay here with me!' Marsh said firmly. 'We've things to discuss.'

'Do come down later!' Jenny smiled. 'Daddy built us our own entertainment room. It's just through the trees, so he can't hear us!'

They made off and the Afghans, at rest on their sides in the shade of the gums, suddenly leapt up in violent excitement, big and powerful enough to send both children flying, which was sometimes the case for all the loving relationship. Jo, by this time, felt she had reached a state where nothing seemed impossible. She stared at Marsh McConnell for a few seconds, then a burst of reaction overcame her.

'There's one particular label you're stuck with, *General*!'

His eyes travelled in a straight line over her face and the iridescent silk blouse. 'What's your problem?'

The oddity of this struck her. 'You're my problem! I'm not a puppet to be pulled on strings!'

'Don't you want to help Anne?' he asked.

'Yes, I do!'

'Well then, what's filling you with this powerful agitation? You're clenching your fist!'

'Instinct!' she said. 'You want to watch out!'

'Imagine! Is that how you feel about me?'

'There's a hateful exhilaration in being with you, yes!' she admitted.

'Remember what they say, Josephine,' he drawled, 'the truth will set you free!'

'I shall be certain to hit you in a minute. Why didn't you tell me?'

'There wasn't time!'

'It doesn't sound at all respectable to me!'

'I have a housekeeper!' he drawled, and for some reason two dull spots of colour burned in her cheeks and the blood moved swiftly through every inch of her.

'I might want to help Anne, but I don't relish going with you. I might be walking into a trap!'

'The truth of the matter is, you're in it already!' His black eyes flicked over her and for a minute Jo was aware of him and nothing else. Not the beauty of the garden and the shining band of the river. Not the lively little blue wrens that hopped about picking up the children's cake crumbs. Her flushed cheeks and her heated blood nearly had her on fire. This man who filled her with resistance had a powerful sexuality, and if her heart hadn't been given for ever she would find herself vulnerable.

'Anyway,' she said, and looked away from him, 'Anne is too unhappy and confused to agree. I feel for her.'

'And you've reached her—I could see that at once. Dave has taken note of it too. I'm not asking anything difficult of you. Look after the children for a month or six weeks and enjoy yourself as well. Naturally I intend to pay you. You may look a million dollars, but I know you're a working girl. Besides, it will give you a breathing space.'

'Oh, thanks!' she said coldly. 'It seems to me you want me out of the way!'

'Do you find that so strange?' he queried.

Jo sighed, disconcerted by the hard light in his eyes. 'I had no idea Blair would be at the shop this morning.'

'Really? The whole effect was one of premeditated passion!'

'You heard him!' she cried.

'And contempt fills me. I find it strange that a woman like you could fall for Blair.'

'Am I so very different from Julie?'

'*Yes!*' he said flatly.

'In any case, Anne won't leave her children,' she went on.

'She will, and you're coming with me.'

'I'd forgotten—you're the General.'

'Then you'd better be careful and obey orders. Anne has to have a complete change of scene. She's only a pale shadow of what she was. It hurts me to see the change in her, and Dave isn't standing up too well either. Don't forget, I know him very well.'

Jo lifted her face towards the wide, glittering river. 'Do you intend to let Julie's marriage go through?'

'Are you thinking of making a fight of it?'

'She loves him and he wants to marry her!'

'Whose case are you arguing?' His black eyes flashed and there was a sparkle of anger in them.

'I wish you'd go away,' she sighed, 'but you won't!'

'No, I won't!' The sun shone directly across his bronze profile and the skin glowed with health. He was really rather superb in a devilish kind of way, but her mind had stored up too many memories of a single face. It swam into sharp focus, thin chiselled features, traditional good looks. She had loved him, and how had he rewarded her, by flinging her to this lion of a man? She had lost something precious and irretrievable when she lost Blair, and anguish flooded her whole being.

Her eyes were like emeralds and her colour was heightened. She knew she was betraying herself, for Marsh's voice had a cutting, contemptuous flavour. 'I usually pride myself on non-interference, but I don't shirk a disagreeable duty either. If Leighton thinks to marry my cousin, I've enough evidence now to persuade her to change her mind.'

'I might love Blair,' she said, feeling giddy and angry, 'but I didn't say I wanted to marry him. *Now!*'

'What are you going to do, wait for me to give him back to you? Didn't it occur to you last night, Julie is afraid of you?'

'She has an extraordinary way of showing it!' snapped Jo.

'She's wondering what you intend to do next.'

'Well, you certainly don't sit around doing that! You charge into the shop, knock Blair down and carry me off!'

'Women have been abducted before,' he said slowly.

'Not in this day and age!'

'I'm trying to save you from tearing yourself to pieces!'

'I can't believe that!' Her hand was shaking violently and she curled it in her lap.

'That's what you're doing, isn't it?' he demanded. 'Leighton's not good enough for you!'

'I don't understand you,' Jo sighed. 'Aren't you on Julie's side?'

'Yes, I am. The thing is, Julie wants him, good or bad. What's more, she has the money to buy him.'

'How despicable!'

'Yes, I think so too,' he returned smoothly. 'Julie's no fool. Don't let those baby blue eyes lead you astray. She wanted Leighton and in her quiet tenacious little way she made that plain. Fortunately he was willing. I think Julie knows very well what she's about.'

'And you've been telling me she needs protection?'

'Protection from *you*, not Leighton. Given a little time she may even handle him. Why I hesitate at all is that I'm certain she's aware of his feelings for you!'

'Don't worry, they're not chronic!' she said bitterly. 'I'm an embarrassment all round!'

'In another six months you'll have forgotten him,' Marsh assured her.

'Oh, *do* shut up!' she sighed. 'Don't ask me to attend the wedding.'

'You may have to. Your Aunt Elizabeth sees you as a beautiful bridesmaid.'

'Dear God!' Jo shuddered.

'You're not vain, are you?'

'Have I any reason to be?' she asked entirely without conceit.

Marsh looked searchingly at her; the warmly tinted olive skin, the beautifully moulded features, the mystery of almond-shaped green eyes and the glossy mass of black hair that had a tinge of plum in the sunlight, and he completely changed the subject.

'Think you'll be able to handle the kids?'

'I'm a woman, aren't I?'

'Very much so, but there's some evidence that a lot of women are hopeless with children.'

Jo glanced at him scathingly from the sides of her iridescent eyes. 'I'll bet I earn every cent you pay me. Actually I'd like to do it for nothing. I'd feel better!'

'I can't let you,' he said.

'If you don't, I won't come. After all, I'm doing it for Anne and Dave, not you. My board and lodging will be more than enough!' she tacked on aggressively. 'I hope we haven't upset Anne any further. I think she's had enough. What do you suppose they're saying?'

'Oh, wondering about you and me! If it helps, let them think this is the beginning of a tender, loving relationship.'

'Now that could never be!' she said jeeringly. 'I have an appointment this afternoon.'

Marsh raised his eyebrows. 'Oh? Doing what?'

'Kindly remember you're not the only man in my life!'

'I pity them!'

'It pleases you to talk like that?'

'I keep remembering Leighton's face,' he said tersely. 'What was he trying to do, get you upstairs?'

'Maybe I would have gone!' Jo lied, infuriated.

'And I'd have broken your neck!'

'Lovely! And I'm answerable to *you*?'

'Quiet!' He held up an imperious hand as if she were no more than a naughty schoolgirl and she found herself gritting her teeth against such outrageous autocracy.

'I'm through when I say I'm through and not a moment before!'

'You're through now!' he said bluntly. 'Anne and Dave are coming back. Seeing the baby-sitters coming to blows hardly inspires confidence!'

Swiftly Jo rearranged her expression and stood up, going towards Anne and touching her arm. 'Forgive me if I upset you, Anne. It was never my intention.'

Anne had been crying, that was evident, from the pinkness of her nose and her puffy lids, but her small face was that of a woman who was moved and deeply touched.

'On the contrary, Jo, I know I've found a good friend in you. I'm sure Marsh was directed in bringing you to us. David and I both think so, and thank you too. If you'll be kind enough to look after the children, we will take that holiday. I owe it to David, and I see now that I really do need one!'

Marsh, on his feet smiling, pulled out her chair. 'Thank God that's settled! Come and sit down again. It's time we made a few plans!'

Over both women's heads, Dave's eloquent blue eyes, so exactly reproduced in his son, communicated to his friend: 'Thanks, pal!'

CHAPTER FOUR

ALL adventures had to be paid for. Jo kept hold of Paddy's little hand, her eyes continually on his pale face. He had been sick twice on the plane and the golden dusting of freckles across his nose were standing out clearly.

'Better, darling?' she asked gently.

'*Worse!*'

'It's excitement!' Jenny offered. 'He's always sick when he's excited.'

They had landed on Malakai's airstrip and their charter pilot, Terry Conrads, a tall, sandy-haired young man with a nice easy manner and a pronounced drawl, was piling their luggage near the entrance to the great silver, shining hangar.

'Who owns the plane over there?' Jenny called to him. 'It's not Uncle Marsh's. Its only got one propeller!'

Terry came back to them dusting his jeans. 'That's Miss Morley's—Philippa Morley's. Her father owns Summerfield, that's the property we flew over on Malakai's north-eastern border. They're pretty big wheels in this part of the world. Pots of money, but they didn't pioneer the country like the Marshall's and the McConnells. Morley bought the property when old Colonel Fullerton died. The old boy's sons were fighter pilots in the Second World War—both of them killed. The old fellow turned into a recluse but he always had time for Marsh. Marsh used to call on him and generally keep an eye on him *and* his property. He's a great bloke, is Marsh. Don't expect *Miss Morley* to be too friendly. Most of us folk aren't good enough for her!' Having delivered himself of that as though driven, Terry then put a big, gentle hand on Paddy's head. 'How are you feeling now, young feller?'

'Worser an' worser!' groaned Paddy, leaning his head against Jo's side.

Anxiously she ran her hand over his face and let it linger on his forehead where his silky brown curls clung damply. 'I think he has a temperature. Perhaps he's coming down with something. Where on earth is Marsh?'

'Unless I'm mistaken, that's him now,' said Terry.

'I can't see anything!'

'All you need is a puff of dust to tell who's coming,' Terry explained. 'We're a good distance from the homestead, but he's expecting us. He would have come for you himself, only that big Texan feller flew in, quite unexpected. One of their top breeders. 'Course, Marsh knew he could trust me with his precious cargo!'

'Yes, and thank you very much, Terry. You looked after us well. It was a very smooth flight. The country looks fantastic from the air—I wish I could have enjoyed it more. A pity about my little pal here. The sooner I get him tucked up in bed the better.'

'Oh, he'll find his legs!' Terry said carelessly. 'It's like young Jenny says, too much excitement. When Marsh arrives, I'll get away. We've been pretty busy of late. If you need someone to fly you out send for me!'

'I'll do that!' Jo smiled, wishing only that Marsh would come so she could get Paddy up to the house. Anne had entrusted her with the care of her children and Jo regarded this as a great responsibility, her anxieties heightened because of the Symons' particular tragedy. Paddy was of a sturdy build like his father and she picked him up, holding him like a native woman over her hip. 'Won't be long, darling!' she comforted him. 'Uncle Marsh will be here then we'll go back to the house. I'll give you a nice cool sponge down and put you into bed.'

'He's all right, isn't he, Jo?' Jenny's anxiety was suddenly in competition with Jo's.

'Yes, dear!' She smiled into the nice, intelligent little

face. 'But he's only a little fellow. Tell me, has he had all
the usual things, measles and mumps?'

'He's had the chickenpox. All the Grade Oners had
the chickenpox!'

'Nothing else?'

'We should have asked Mummy!'

'Here's Marsh now.' Terry broke into their contem-
plation of Paddy's childhood ills. 'And Miss Morley.
Trust her not to want to miss out on anything. I'll say my
goodbyes now, folks—she won't want me here. Take
care!'

Like the little gentleman he was Paddy lifted his head
to say goodbye and add his polite thanks. Terry saluted
them and swerved away to the Cessna, coming to a halt
beside it for all the world like a chauffeur standing to
attention. It seemed odd to Jo, but it wasn't her place to
make a comment. Jenny wanted to run forward towards
the moving vehicle, but Jo grabbed her by the hand.
'Stay here, dear!' she warned, feeling exactly like a
mother hen. 'Wait until it comes to a complete stop. I
wish I had my sunglasses, the light is blinding.'

'Shall I get them?' Jenny offered. 'They're in your
shoulder bag.'

'No, it doesn't matter now.' The Range Rover came to
a stop near the end of the hangar, then Marsh was out of
it, waving a hand to Terry and coming towards their
own little group. A young woman moved lightly beside
him, almost dancing to keep up, her auburn hair glittering like a flame in the brilliant sunshine.

Just for once, Jo thought dismally, I'd like to meet a
woman of my own height! Philippa Morley couldn't
have been more than five two or three, but very nicely
rounded like a pocket Venus. Her black jeans fitted her
like a second skin and her high, firm breasts beneath the
expensive T-shirt played havoc with the film star's face
that was transferred on to it. As they drew close Jo could
see the redhead's fragile white skin and the topaz-

coloured eyes, a broad forehead tapering to a pointed chin, a small pouting mouth which still managed to convey an attitude of no compromise. A conclusion if she cared, which she *didn't* Jo assured herself, not to be tempted by Philippa Morley's man, and it was obvious he was travelling right alongside her. The thing to do was to keep calm. She was here to look after the children and she had to make it plain from the beginning. She had no intention of creating problems or complicating things, neither did she particularly care if she made a favourable impression on Marsh McConnell's possible fiancée.

Jo released her firm hold on Jenny and the little girl flew towards Marsh, who scooped her up easily. Poor little Paddy lifted his head trying to concentrate on Uncle Marsh's progress, but it proved too much of an effort, and his hot face soon found its way back to the comfort of Jo's neck.

'What's wrong, Jo?' Marsh was beside her, taller, broader, even more striking than she remembered, lifting Paddy out of her aching arms.

'I think he's coming down with something. He's running a temperature.'

'Then we'd better get him back to the house. How was he on the trip?'

'He was sick twice,' Jo told him.

'Good God!' he muttered. 'How's my poor little mate?'

'All right, Uncle Marsh!' Paddy said, gallantly worried he was going to be sick again.

Jo glanced quickly towards Marsh's companion and surprised an expression of blame and impatience in the round topaz eyes. Marsh was still staring into Paddy's pallid little face, but he looked up briefly to introduce them.

'Philippa Morley, Jo Adams. You'll be seeing quite a bit of each other.'

Neither girl smiled and Philippa looked into Jo's face

with bright accusing eyes. 'You didn't give him anything silly to eat on the plane, did you? Chocolate or potato chips?'

'Negative to both!' Jo said shortly, taking an instant dislike to the younger girl.

'Let's get him back to the house,' said Marsh, missing the clash. 'I'll have to have a word with Terry.' He walked away to the charter pilot with Paddy firmly wrapped in his strong arms. There was a minute's conversation, then Terry waved and climbed into the Cessna.

'I want Jo to sit with me!' Paddy announced as Philippa moved towards the front seat.

'All three of us will fit neatly in the back!' Before anyone could move Jo had opened the rear door and propelled Jenny across the seat, then turned to take Paddy out of Marsh's arms.

'It might be an idea if we wait a moment!' Marsh said quietly. 'I think he's going to be sick.'

'Here, give him to me!' Jo moved swiftly as Marsh set the boy down and in the next second Paddy began to retch. Jo held his head and when the spasms stopped wiped his clammy little face with the clean handkerchief Marsh passed her. 'My poor little boy!' she soothed, holding him gently.

Jenny in the Range Rover began to cry, anxious and totally ignored. Marsh looked in at her and put out his hand. 'Be a good girl now, Jenny. Move over and help Jo with your brother. We'll have him up to the house in no time.'

'He's not going to *die*, is he?' she asked fearfully, hearing the sound of her mother's weeping in her ears.

'Of course not!' Jo and Marsh broke in together, sounding equally appalled.

'You *are* a silly little girl!' Phillipa observed crisply, turning back to Jenny with a quelling glance. 'Little boys are always being sick!'

'Jenny knows that only too well!' said Jo shortly, finding such a remark completely unnecessary. It seemed doubly important to her to show the children extra love with their mother and father away. She settled back against the seat holding Paddy's small compact body protectively against her, Jenny rammed up against her side, although there was plenty of room and the afternoon sun struck powerfully through the wrap-around windows.

Marsh held her gaze with his own. 'Philippa doesn't know much about the family,' he pointed out mildly, then he turned away to stow the luggage before climbing into the driver's seat. He looked even more notorious in his everyday clothes: close-fitting jeans and high leather boots, his khaki shirt open to expose a tangle of hair on his broad, darkly-tanned chest, a cream wide-brimmed slouch hat tilted forward rakishly on a head that had blown into black curls, his hat circled with a beautifully marked snakeskin band.

Even with the weight of her responsibilities on her Jo could still catch the unmistakable pulsing of feeling that emanated from Philippa. No doubt such splendid male virility would make the blood race to most women's heads, but to Jo's jaundiced eye he looked larger than life size, a big, bold, bad adventurer. Only Blair had put her heart in a tumult, and he would look incongruous in jeans and a bush shirt. Philippa kept darting little appraising looks over her shoulder. Jo felt crushed and none too fresh, having dealt with poor little Paddy, and she could almost have laughed imagining the thoughts that must have been running through Philippa's head. Under that delectable chocolate coating she had the notion that Philippa was a very tough cookie indeed. It was perfectly absurd of her to worry about Jo as a possible competitor. In fact she could scratch her off the list right away. Marsh McConnell was simply a man she could sharpen her wits on. She didn't have to defend herself from him. It was perfectly absurd!

Through the light woodland or natural bushland, she could see the white glimmer of buildings. There were bungalows surrounded by gardens, what seemed to be a small playing park for children, administration buildings and a huge sales shed. It was a settlement in itself and the space and freedom, the pure, dry invigorating air, lent it a wonderful magic. Even Paddy stirred against her and lifted his head. 'Isn't it beautiful, Aunty Jo?'

He had taken to calling her that quite naturally, and she was astounded at the surge of love she felt for another woman's child. 'It is indeed, my pet. I only wish you were feeling better so we could enjoy it!'

'Oh, do look at the bougainvillaea,' Jenny insisted. 'There are mountains of it!'

And so there were. It seemed to spill everywhere, clinging in a glorious riot of colour to almost everything that was standing, buildings and trees, the common magenta and the introduced modern hybrids, white, scarlet, pink and violet and a beautiful orange and bronze trained over a great trellis like a Japanese tori gate that spanned the drive. There were stands of wiry-branched casuarinas, towering gums and feathery acacias and melaleucas, and almost as prolific the beautiful, showy bauhinias, the orchid trees, their bare branches covered in great flowers in a variety of colours. Splendid ornamental succulents from South Africa and Mexico thrived in the hot, dry conditions, spring flowers appeared on the brilliantly flowering cacti.

As they drew nearer to the homestead, the savannah gave way to a more cultivated setting with a broad expanse of lawn and bountiful gardens where two aboriginal boys were actively digging and sprinklers played out fountains of water in shimmering cascades. There was even an ornamental lake some hundreds of yards long floating a waxy burden of nymphaea and the exquisite blue lotus, the sacred flower of the Pharaohs. It was fantastic to find a place like this anywhere and quite dizzying on the fringe of the desert. It was actually getting a little beyond Jo, who hadn't really grasped the vast scale of the place and had in fact been feeling so unsettled and forsaken to think much about Malakai. It began to strike her, as it would increasingly in the weeks ahead, that Marsh McConnell lived somewhat like a Pharaoh himself in his male-dominated world.

They started to climb and the house rose before them, typifying man and his castle. Jo was betrayed into a gasp. It was bigger, much bigger than she expected, a mansion in the wilds, big enough to house an army and strong enough to stand as a fortress, which of course it had done during the Black Wars. Marsh turned his head far from accidentally and caught the bemused expression on her face. He might even have guessed at her thoughts. She would never be able to separate him from his house and his land again. There was a kind of exultancy in both of them, a grandeur and a strength that actually moved her.

Paddy felt her quick intake of breath and lay back against her heart, satisfied. Jo loved Malakai just as much as Jenny and he did. 'We're here!' Jenny sighed, like the beginning of a great adventure.

'And it's paradise!' Jo said sincerely.

This earned her a sharp look of increased speculation from Philippa. The topaz eyes glittered, giving fair warning, but the tone was honeyed: 'And we do hope you'll enjoy your visit!'

Her choice of words was deliberate and even the children seemed to get the message, Jenny going so far as to crinkle up her nose. Jo glanced at Philippa to see if she had seen, but she had already turned back to address some private remark to Marsh. Jo missed his reply; she was too busy looking at the house. As they pulled up a short distance from the front steps, two members of the household staff came out, a man and a woman, part aboriginal and part European. The man, impeccably turned out in a kind of uniform of short-sleeved white shirt and white trousers, went to collect the luggage and the woman came towards them, a smile spread all over her motherly face.

'Welcome!' she said in a broad drawl. A woman past middle age but a strong woman, within and without, her skin and her hair and her eyes faded by the sun. 'Great kangaroos! What's wrong with the little feller?'

'Jo,' Marsh said, smiling, 'this is Ellen, my housekeeper and an indispensable member of my team. If there's anything you want to know at any time, from childbirth to snakebite and custard through to crêpes, ask Ellen. There's no little problem she can't untangle!'

'How are you there, Jo?' Ellen came a few steps forward, wiping her hand on her apron before she extended her hand to Jo. 'Been making scones, you know. There's no end to the number they put away at smoko!' Her faded blue eyes were rapidly assessing the young woman before her. She hadn't known quite what to expect, having little experience of city-bred women, but she very nearly drew a sigh of relief. Jo met her eyes directly and her handshake was nearly as strong as her own. No problems there! the blue eyes seemed to say. Ellen Hays was a great one for spotting capability. This young woman would prove a useful ally and she would be sensible in the Big Country. Malakai, for all its beauty and wild grandeur, didn't favour the stupid or reckless. More than one guest on the property had become lost before a search party brought them back.

Quickly Jo explained how sick Paddy had been and Ellen, all concern, hurried them back into the house, shepherding Jo and the children ahead. There was no time to admire the interior, but Jo was overwhelmingly conscious of magnificence very much to be seen. A deep wide hallway divided the house into two wings and a polished hardwood stairway sprang up to lead off on either side to the first floor gallery and bedrooms that

were as big as many a modern living room. One painting
in the gallery caught her moving eyes and she thought
for a moment it was Marsh, only the subject had blue
eyes and was wearing the uniform of a Wing-Com-
mander in the Royal Australian Air Force. He looked
very dashing indeed and his vivid face and lean body
almost leapt from the canvas.

'Master Gavin!' said Ellen, and it sounded like a
tribute. 'Marsh's father. He had a very distinguished
career in the Second World War. Shot down and
escaped. Had all sorts of adventures. Married an English
bride—or a mixture of French and English, for she had
a French side to her family. A grand lady is Mrs Mc-
Connell!'

'Yes, I've met her.'

'Went to pieces after Master Gavin was killed,' Ellen
went on. 'Shock put those silver wings in her hair. Quite
natural, *I* know. Not that it doesn't make her look all
the more handsome. She couldn't stay here at any rate.
It was a great tragedy. We had some visitors here for a
week-end, they were always entertaining, and the master
was shot accidentally—by a friend. My God, what a day
that was! Just a dreadful freak accident. The poor man
had a nervous breakdown afterwards, but the family
never held him to blame—publicly, that is. I've never
forgotten my poor lady's raving. Stumbled over a fence
and the gun went off. We're all fighting the effects of it in
our own way, even Marsh. He adored his father and
there was no one in the world for Master Gavin like his
son. We all thought he was going to live to be a hundred.
I mean, he did come through the war.

'Ah well! ...' Ellen paused with her hand on the door-
knob. 'Young Paddy and Jenny in here. We moved
another bed in—I thought it would be cosier to have
them together. The rooms are so big they might get lost
and lonely all by themselves. This room adjoins your
own across a little sitting room.' She walked across and

opened another door and Jo and the children went into
the room, Jo depositing Paddy temporarily in a deep
armchair. Jenny ventured a sweet smile at the housekeeper, who responded in kind.

'How do you like this, young lady?'

'Oh, it's beautiful! This isn't the room we had before.'

'So you remember?'

'Of course.'

'And what a bonny child you've grown, the living spit
of your mother. How is she now?'

'She'd be in America!' Jenny said grandly.

Jo went to one of the canopied beds that occupied the
centre of the room, turning back the quilt. The floor was
parqueted, scattered with Persian rugs, and a huge
gilded mirror stood over the white marble fireplace,
filled now with a beautiful luxuriant fern in a copper pot,
the new fronds a striking bright red. All of the furniture
was Victorian, its solid opulence suited to the scale of
the room, but there was nothing heavy or dark in the
atmosphere. The wallpaper had been renewed in a light
and airy modern design and the french doors stood
open to the veranda which, like the ground floor, ran the
length of the house and protected the interior from the
heat of the sun.

Ellen bustled over to help Jo. "You'll find everything
you need. Barney will have your things up directly. One
of the girls can help you unpack if you like—give them
something to do. There's linen on the beds and plenty of
towels in the bathroom. Your room is the nicest outside
the master suite. It has its own bathroom and there's a
bathroom for the children just across the hall.'

Jo was deftly stripping off Paddy's clothes to his
underpants, feeling his heated skin. 'I think I'll give him
a whole aspirin,' she decided.

'I'll get it.' Ellen walked through the rooms and returned in a minute with the tablet and a glass of water.
'If he doesn't pick up quickly we'll get the doctor on the

radio. He can fly in if needs be.' She reached over and ran her own hand over Paddy's face and limbs. 'Yes, he has a temperature all right. I shouldn't be surprised if we see some spots coming out.'

'Oh, I hope not!' wailed Jenny, seeing herself trapped inside.

Paddy took the aspirin like a good boy and lay back on the cool sheets. 'Better have a bucket ready just in case. I'll send one up. Meanwhile, use that towel. Don't worry, little feller,' she said to Paddy's unblinking eyes. 'We'll have you up and about in no time!'

Paddy smiled, showing some of his usual potent charm. 'I couldn't bear to stay in bed!'

'That's the spirit!' Ellen beamed. 'Let's see if you keep that aspirin down. Meantime I'll go flatten some lemonade. Nothing solid until your tummy settles!' At the door she turned about, giving an approving nod to Barney's slim figure as he deposited their luggage just inside the door. 'This is Barney. He controls our house boys.'

Barney looked up and grinned as if really amused, his great liquid black eyes dancing. 'Miss Ellen's really in charge!'

'All the same, I rely on you, Barney!'

Barney smiled across at Jo and the children. 'Please ask me if there's anything you need.' His voice was very melodious and soft and in the way of his race he really understood children. They all returned the friendly smile and Barney dismissed himself shyly.

'I'd better ask Nara to come up and help you,' Ellen said briskly, and in another second had followed Barney down the passageway.

Nara turned out to be a lovely little lubra with gleaming café-au-lait skin and a head full of tight coal-black curls. She wore a pale blue pinafore and from the unusual exotica of her features and her skin tone it was obvious she had a mixture of antecedents. Her nose was

straight and fine with only a slight widening of the
nostrils and her slender body and limbs were more
rounded and substantial than those of a full-blooded
aboriginal woman. Jo and the children took to her immediately and she proved very deft at the job of un-
packing.

With that task taken away from her, Jo gave Paddy a
nice cool sponge down, then sat down on the bed holding
his hand. Jenny was chattering away like a budgie,
following Nara back and forth and asking her questions.
When Paddy felt a little bit better Jo decided she would
have a quick shower and change her clothes. She felt
marked by their trip.

'How is he now?' A voice came behind them and Jo
turned to see Philippa advancing into the room as if she
owned it, a faint frown between her brows, and a green
plastic bucket in her hand. 'Mrs Hays said to give you
this.'

'Thank you. He's a little better now.' Jo stood up
quickly, conscious of the barrier of hostility between
them. She took the bucket which Philippa relinquished
with a moue of distaste and placed it beside the bed.
Nara came back through the sitting room and Philippa's
eyes glinted over her.

'Have you finished?'

'Yes, missy!' Nara said sweetly, bearing up philo-
sophically under the tone.

'Then you may go!'

'But I was talking to her!' Jenny ran in to remonstrate.

'What about?' Philippa's perfect nostrils flared.

'About legends, actually!' said Jenny, looking Philippa squarely in the eye.

'That's not her job. Don't go filling the children's
heads with nonsense, Nara!'

'It's not nonsense!' Jenny protested sincerely, not in
the least scared like the lubra. 'I'm very interested in the
Dreamtime myths. For instance, did you know about

Tirlta and the Flowers of Blood? That's Sturt's desert pea. Dad said to learn as many as I can. It would make me a much brighter girl.'

Philippa turned away with a tinge of dislike. 'You're certainly outspoken!' she snapped.

'Daddy said children don't have to be seen and not heard any more!'

There was a painful little pause and Jo jumped into it, looking across at the silent Nara and the unusually aggressive Jenny. 'Perhaps you could take Jenny downstairs, Nara, and look after her for a little while.'

Nara bobbed her glossy head until the curls shook. 'Pleased to, ma'am!' She took Jenny by the hand and both girls skirted Philippa in a wide semicircle, with Jenny mumbling something out of the corner of her mouth when they were barely out of earshot.

'What a disagreeable child!' Philippa said indignantly, not at all sure she hadn't heard 'bitch!'

Paddy tried to struggle up, looking for a fight, and Jo had to press him back into the pillow. 'You're not very diplomatic, are you? The children are delightful.'

'The girl will make a proper little battle-axe, if you ask me,' snapped Philippa. 'Marsh is so very kindhearted!'

'You don't sound sure if this pleases you or not!'

'On the contrary, I would have offered to come over and look after them for what little time they'll be here. I can't think why Marsh didn't ask me. He knows perfectly well I'd refuse him nothing!' The topaz eyes seemed to glitter balefully. 'I imagine he employed you?'

'Not at all!' Joe was heartily glad to say it. 'Like Marsh, I'm simply doing a favour for a friend.'

'And seeing Malakai while you're at it. I must say you look the last person in the world I'd have chosen as a nanny!' Philippa's piercing gaze swept Jo from head to foot, noting with displeasure the older girl's immense chic. Her expert eye knew exactly how much that collarless silk shirt had cost, the tobacco-brown slacks, even the gold hoop earrings and the chain around Jo's neck. Fashion might always favour tall, lean women, Philippa considered thoughtfully, but she believed emphatically that men much preferred curvaceousness. She ran her hands over her own rounded hips, seeking her very attractive image in the large gilded mirror. It obviously reassured her, and Jo could have smiled. She didn't know why Philippa was going to so much trouble to get her message across and she would have liked to inform her that she didn't share her taste in men—Marsh McConnell, for example.

'Do you think you'll manage?' Philippa asked derisively.

Jo leaned over and felt Paddy's cheek, noting the cooling of his skin. 'I think so.'

'Have you experience of children, then?'

'Actually no. I was an only child. No brothers or sisters. No big happy family, but I'm very fond of children.'

'Then how did Marsh come to ask you?' Philippa continued to probe, her eyes narrowing slightly.

'He was really quite clever about it,' Jo explained. 'He sprang it on me!'

This time the reddish-brown brows shot up. 'Come, surely you put it to him?'

'Not at all. He was a very sweeping personality. He carried us all along with him. You look as though you find something wrong with it?'

Philippa gave a rather crude little laugh.

'Do you blame me? Marsh always has women after him. That's common knowledge!'

'Indeed? It's grand to be popular!'

Philippa's kitten face set like a stone. 'How long have you known him?'

'This is actually the fourth time we've met,' said Jo.

'I don't believe you!'

'It's true, though!' Jo was beginning to get headachey with the endless questions, but at least the conversation was taking Paddy's mind off his troubles. His blue eyes were like saucers, pleased that Aunty Jo was handling the other lady effectively.

'Well, you're good-looking,' said Philippa, 'I can't deny it!'

Jo turned her body slowly to look steadily at the other girl. 'Miss Morley, I'd really like to reassure you. You may find Marsh McConnell tremendously magnetic, but I don't think I ever will.'

'There's no hurry!'

Marsh's dry tone surprised both of them, sounding vibrantly across the room.

'Well, there it is!' Jo said wryly. 'You can't win 'em all!'

'You bet you can!' Far from looking ungratified by her comment, there was a tolerant humour in his very black eyes. He even appeared to relish such unaccustomed indifference. He touched Philippa's shoulder lightly, then walked across to the bed, looking down at the wide-eyed child. 'I do believe you're looking better?'

'A little bit, Uncle Marsh. Remember how we used to play hide and seek?'

'It seems a shame we can't do it now, but tomorrow will be fine.'

'This is a beaut house!' commented Paddy, resettling on his pillows.

'And plenty of places to hide is one of its charms,' Marsh pointed out. 'I feel better you're better. When you're up and about, so we won't be too selfish, I'll arrange for Nara to look after you occasionally to give Jo a break.'

'She's not going away now?' Paddy asked uneasily.

'Oh no!'

'I couldn't possibly!' Jo seconded.

Philippa was staring from one to the other as though

trying to convince herself of something. 'Why you didn't ask me, I'll never know!' she said crossly.

Marsh turned to her smoothly. 'I simply didn't think you'd have the time. Besides, minding children is uphill work and there's precious little of you!'

Jo couldn't quite agree on that, but she said nothing, noting that Philippa coloured up looked enticingly pretty. The topaz eyes flashed and the round breasts swelled.

'You know I'd do anything for you!'

'Well, come down and join me in a long cold drink. Jo,' he glanced across at her kindly, 'you're coming down to dinner, of course?'

She didn't even hesitate. 'If it's all the same to you, I'd prefer to have something here. I won't feel happy until Paddy's fever has broken. The aspirin has brought his temperature down, but it could rise again during the evening.'

'As you wish. I'll tell Ellen.'

She looked up anxiously and pushed the heavy fall of hair away from her face. 'If it's no trouble!'

'No trouble at all.'

Philippa's pleasure was indescribable. 'In that case I think I'll stay on till morning. You won't want to have dinner on your own.'

'Why, sure!' Marsh half smiled and looked down into Philippa's triangular little face. 'We've any number of beds to accommodate you!'

Philippa blushed and gave a breathless little gurgle and Jo, understanding her line of thought, turned away. Momentarily she had had the uninvited notion that Marsh McConnell would make a mighty fine lover. Why she thought that seemed remarkable, considering the judgment she had already handed down. He was a superb animal, that was it; a powerful beautifully co-ordinated male animal. His sexual aura was effortless, tossed off like a blue flame, and Philippa's eyes were a polished mirror to reflect her desire. It was sickening, and Jo looked away from them pointedly. Paddy sighed dramatically and Jo was inclined to think he was improving.

After they had gone and the little boy's eyelids had started to droop, Jo walked to the french doors that led out on to the veranda. The light was still dazzling and would remain so until the brief twilight. A golden haze lay over the garden and settled on the trees so that the leaves glittered like knives. How beautiful it was! She was a little astonished at the sudden burst of happiness that lifted her heart. Stretching far, far away, as far as the eye could see was a great Outback station, Malakai. If she could throw off her feelings, her absorption with the past, she could enjoy it, take steps to start a new life.

She had heard nothing from Blair, but she had seen Julie twice in the week before she had come away, both times at Aunt Elizabeth's. For the first time in a very long time, Aunt Elizabeth had shown a deep disappointment in Jo. It was one thing to foster a new romance and quite another to leave Blair in the lurch. She hadn't bothered to hide her annoyance. It had poured down like the rain from heaven. In a way it was even merciful, because Jo preferred her to think that than guess at her misery. Uncle Joss had guessed at once. There had always been a silent communion between them.

One way and the other it had been a very uncomfortable ten days, but at least she had accomplished something, and she marvelled she had done it. Julie had squeezed her hand and told her in a quick, nervous voice how 'understanding' it was of Jo to realise she might like bridesmaids all her own petite height. Aunt Elizabeth, feeling Jo had sacrificed her son's interests, for once had nothing to say. How Jo was going to get out of attending the actual ceremony she didn't at this stage know. She had loved Blair far too long to take her mind off him now. Everything about him had been beautiful to her. She could see his weaknesses now and it helped, but old habits died hard. Especially loving. She hated what he had done to her—yes, *hated* it, but she longed for the old days. Blair had wrecked her life to make a new one of his own, but for good or bad he was in her blood.

Paddy behind her was gently dozing and Jo continued to stand at the long windows staring out. A glorious sunset came and went, lighting the world to crimson and rose-gold. She could see it colouring the very air. Masses of birds of glowing plumage homed in to the sanctuaries, shrieking and whistling; a brief moment when the world turned to a mysterious mauve, then dark.

Paddy's temperature rose again as the evening progressed and it wasn't until shortly before midnight that his fever broke. Jenny, tired out after the long trip, slept right through Jo's ministrations to her brother, and Jo was grateful for it.

'Better, dear?' She smiled gently into Paddy's astonishing blue eyes. Gossamer wisps of damp brown hair clung to his childish brow, and he threw a quick grateful look at her.

'I'm nice and clean now. Look at Jenny. She looks happy—she's smiling!'

'You will be too in the morning. I'm going to leave this soft light on and I'll be close at hand.'

Paddy nodded his head but was prevented from answering by his exhaustion. To Jo's intense relief, he turned on his side and went to sleep. Whatever had troubled him apparently was leaving him and Jo adjusted the lamp, staring vaguely around the room as if she had emerged from some sort of crisis. There was a wonderful old chaise-longue in her own room, but she hadn't a hope of shifting it and now Paddy was sleeping so peacefully she didn't dare shift him into her own bed. The only thing she could do was keep hopping up and

For *YOU*
a top-favourite
Mills & Boon 🌹
Romance
FREE

— just for telling us which Mills & Boon love story you have enjoyed reading MOST in the past 6 months!

HOW TO CLAIM *YOUR* FREE BOOK

Simply fill-in the details below, cut-off *whole page* and post TODAY!

To: MILLS AND BOON READER SERVICE, PO. BOX 236, 14 Sanderstead Road, South Croydon, Surrey, CR2 9PU.

Please write in BLOCK LETTERS below

The Mills & Boon love story I have most enjoyed during the past 6 months is:—

TITLE

AUTHOR

Please send my FREE Mills & Boon romance to:—

NAME (Mrs/Miss)

ADDRESS

CITY/TOWN

COUNTY   POST CODE

Offer applies only in UK and Eire   XXXX/4R78

CUT-OFF WHOLE PAGE HERE AND POST TODAY – *NO STAMP NEEDED!*

RC/4/78/RS

down to check on him through the night.

Jenny gave a muffled little sigh in her sleep and outside in the hallway the big old grandfather clock struck midnight. Probably the others were long in bed. Jo had seen Ellen and Marsh several times before and after dinner, but Philippa had neglected to look in on the little patient again. It came to her suddenly that the shatteringly empty feeling in her stomach was really hunger. She had paid no attention to the delicious dinner Ellen had prepared for her and Nara had brought up. She was even a little lightheaded. She crossed the width of the room and went to the door, opening it up. The hallway still burned with soft lights and there were some lights on downstairs. She knew perfectly well had she been at home she would have made herself coffee and toast. She could still do it if Ellen was up. It would help her through her night watch. The intensity of her devotion to Anne's children was an integral part of her nature and an attribute that worked for and against her.

There was silence right through the great house and she walked down the divided stairway pausing at the first landing. 'Ellen?' she called softly.

No answer.

She leaned over the banisters the better to see and there was Marsh staring up at her. 'I see now why some men get married!' he drawled.

'I beg your pardon?'

The brilliant black eyes flashed over her and in spite of herself Jo felt disturbed.

'Do you always look like that when you're going to bed?' he went on.

'I might sleep on my own,' she whispered vehemently, 'but I like to look nice!'

'That's the understatement of the year!'

Her heart gave that curious bump again, but she shook off the feeling. 'I'm as well covered as if I wore an evening gown. Probably more!'

'Oh, my *dear*!'

His black eyebrows arched and she could have smacked his dark mocking face with pleasure. He was doing it deliberately. It wasn't as though she favoured transparency. Her nightgown and matching wrap were both silk crêpe-de-chine with lavish insets of lace and no deep plunging V such as Philippa might have shown off to advantage. She was actually quite modest in that department. 'Anyway, I didn't expect to find you here,' she said virtuously.

'This *is* my home. Paddy all right?'

'Sleeping peacefully, thank the good Lord!'

'I wonder what was the matter with him?'

Jo shook her head. 'I don't know. I'm only hoping he'll be his bright self in the morning. Such a thing to happen, and he's only just away from his mother!'

'You managed,' Marsh pointed out.

'Team work. I had help!' She stood there poised for a moment, her face softened, not actually seeing him, then she murmured 'Goodnight', and went to go. Her wrap caught on the polished dome of the handrail and drew back to reveal a slender, very feminine silhouette.

He gave an entranced whistle and she stormed at him, 'Do stop that! You're making me nervous!'

'Not half as nervous as you're making me. Tell me, what did you want?'

'I was hungry, if you must know it!'

'In the middle of the night?'

'I didn't eat much of dinner!' she justified herself.

'Then come on down. It's insane to be frightened of me.'

'My God, I should think so!'

He gave a growled laugh in his throat and Jo whirled around saying, 'I'll just check again on Paddy, then I'll join you.'

'Please don't change. What would you like?'

'Oh, something light. Coffee and toast.'

'Won't that keep you awake?'

'That's the idea!' she answered.

'Then let me get it for you. A midnight feast!' He bowed suavely and for an instant she saw his French ancestry. He really did it rather well.

Five minutes later she was seated at the large circular table in the kitchen visibly thawing by the minute, the delicious aroma of freshly ground coffee assisting the atmosphere.

'What a wonderful old house this is!' she commented.

'*I* like it!' Deftly Marsh set out cups and saucers.

'The kitchen's nearly as big as a ballroom. Like me to remodel it?'

'Ellen *may* be interested.'

'Just let me sit here a minute and think of it. You have everything going for you, the size, that superb old fireplace. What you really need is an island work centre, a different placement of equipment. I could work wonders and it would help Ellen enormously. Leave it to me,' she said triumphantly, 'I'm very diplomatic!'

'Not with the Boss!' he said dryly, 'but Ellen's sold on you. You've only just arrived and you're redecorating my home!'

'Some things just come naturally!' Jo said absent-mindedly, her green eyes skipping all around the room. 'Don't worry about the money I spend, it will be well worth it in the long run. Careful planning will make Ellen's job a lot easier.'

'Here, drink your coffee before you change everything!' Marsh sat down opposite her, his black eyes dominating his face.

'Thank you.' She had the grace to go pink, accepting the whipped cream but no sugar. 'It's only a suggestion. The last thing I want to do is remake your home.'

'What about *me*?' he grinned.

'And put myself in jeopardy?'

'That's the last straw after what I know about *you*!'

he said sharply, his dark face reflecting his scorn.

Jo sighed. 'Are we going to be buddies or not?' she asked patiently. 'I have to stay alert so I can keep an eye on Paddy.'

'No need to overdo it!'

'That's the way I am.'

'Yes, I know!' he said with sarcastic charm.

Now she was piqued. 'Damn it, don't keep harping on one reckless act!'

'So you've put Leighton out of your mind.'

'I may have!' she said moodily, and treated herself to a little sugar. It might have some value in keeping her calm.

'You can't promise everlasting devotion to Julie's man!' he said smoothly, obviously needling her.

'I saw him first!' she said crossly.

'That should only make you realise he's decided his life.'

'And good luck to him!' Jo said with enormous difficulty.

'Don't sulk like a child. Drink up!'

Her face was downcast and her skin flawless within the dark clouds of her hair. 'I'm afraid I upset Aunt Elizabeth!' she told him.

'Oh, how?'

Jo shrugged almost defiantly, more hurt than she would ever admit at Aunt Elizabeth's attitude. 'She couldn't see how I could possibly leave Blair in the lurch!'

'*Mothers!*' he groaned, not the least bit politely.

'She doesn't even know I've left him for good.'

His black eyes flicked her face and he threw up his head like a spirited thoroughbred. 'All this talk of Blair!' he said impatiently. 'She obviously ruined him. Don't do that to your sons!'

'I'd better get a move on!' she said wryly, because the matter concerned her greatly.

Unexpectedly Marsh's face softened and his voice was quick and amused. 'I'm sure there isn't a man alive who wouldn't hasten to oblige you, including that blackguard Blair!'

'Oh, don't call him that!' She put up a hand and tousled her hair.

'What esteemed word would you substitute?' he enquired.

'Offhand I can't think of a single contribution. Never admit a weakness, that's my motto. Why did you put the cream away? I'd like another cup.'

She stood up quickly, seeking relief from talk of Blair, but he reached the huge double refrigerator before her. They were very close and she began to think there was something radically wrong with her. Electricity was crackling to and fro between them, feathering across her skin. It was absurd and disturbing, yet it held her like a silly moth in the centre of a web.

Marsh turned his head sideways and his eyes travelled over her. 'My mother warned me about fast women!'

'It's sweet of you to feel like that, but I'm not out to seduce you.'

'Not worth it?'

'Too late!' she said sweetly, misreading his expression.

'Yes?' Those disconcerting black eyes rested on her face, and for some reason every muscle in her body contracted violently. 'Let's try anyway!' He reached for her and caught her by the shoulders, drawing her to him in an almost balletic movement.

Flares of reaction were shooting through her too strong to be ignored. He seemed to like overpowering her and he was big enough to do it, his tall, rangy body like some perfect machine. 'This is absurd!' she said tersely.

'It won't be for long. I mean, you've taken such pains to come down in your nightie!'

'You know perfectly well...' Her voice quivered and cut out. 'If you're going to kiss me,' she gritted, 'get it over!'

'I'm not going to kiss you at all!'

'Oh beauty, oh joy!' Her vivid face was a study in feline mockery.

'There'll be plenty of opportunities!' he added, grinning.

'Depend on me to thwart them!'

Unexpectedly he laughed, his teeth beautifully white against his dark copper face. 'Whatever would you do if I decided I wanted you?'

'Jump from the roof!'

'Shall we take a wager on that?'

'If it will make you happy!' Jo's green eyes defied him and there was a bright recklessness in her that matched his own temper, yet his face was full of shadows.

'Don't you see you're making things harder?' he said softly.

'Blame it on the witching hour!'

He stared at her for a minute but he didn't speak a word, and fancifully Jo thought of herself as Persephone about to be carried off by the King of the Underworld. His eyes were the blackest and most brilliant she had ever seen.

'For God's sake!' she said abruptly just as he bent his head and touched his mouth to the side of her neck. Just a touch and she went weak from the shock, trembling as if he was maltreating her. She couldn't trust herself a minute longer. This was something fierce like fire, elemental and never sought. Rather stupidly she arched away from him and his mouth trailed to the curve of her breast. Nothing she had ever felt in her life equalled it, and it seemed shocking and disloyal.

'I knew all along you were no gentlemen!' she whispered fiercely.

'Are you sure? I'm not insulting you. Leighton did that!'

Jo struggled wildly, but he parried her easily, holding her so she had to go quiet. 'You've got the devil of a temper!' he observed.

'You should understand about *that*!'

'What I don't understand is how you can be such a fool!'

Unexpectedly she drooped against him like a spent child. 'Please, Marsh!' Her voice shook, then broke.

Just as suddenly his hard strength became gentleness and something that almost seemed like tenderness, but of course she couldn't be sure of it. 'You hurt me!' she whispered in a kind of anguish.

'Here, show me!'

'No. You're dangerous and you override people!'

'One needs to sometimes. Don't look so endangered. I didn't hurt you at all. In fact I'm trying to be patient. What on earth was it we were after?'

'Cream, but it doesn't matter!'

'Have it. You'll feel better.'

Jo went back to her chair as if it were some place of security. 'I'm not accustomed to rough handling!' she persisted as though seeking an apology.

'My lady, forgive me!' he said instantly. 'You're the only woman I know who can't seem to see me as a prize!'

'You've a great deal of vanity!' She was looking at him as if she had never seen him before in her life.

'Nearer home, *money*!' he said rather cynically.

'How silly! I'm compelled to tell you, you fall far short of my requirements.'

'God, I hope so!' he retorted sarcastically. 'I'm not exactly blind to your many faults!'

Her head flew up and her eyes glittered like a cat's, but footsteps in the quiet held her tense and silent. In another minute Philippa swished into the kitchen wrapped in bright suspicion and the final word in sexy night attire, braking abruptly when she saw Jo. Many were the tricks women got up to, said her outraged expression.

'Hi there!' Jo raised her eyes.

'I thought I'd better check why all the lights were on,' Philippa said icily.

'I usually leave them until I turn in,' Marsh said mildly, still standing by the refrigerator door. 'Want a cup of coffee?'

'Don't be silly, not at this hour!' She glared at Jo and despite herself Jo gave a little chuckle.

'I had to have it,' she explained. 'I was almost done in!'

'Surely the boy's asleep now?'

'To my enormous relief. I was really worried.'

'I'm sure!'

'It's a responsibility, looking after children,' Jo answered, trying to be patient.

'Sit down, Phil!' Marsh ordered abruptly and evidently she saw sense, for the grimness on her kitten face faded into mischievousness.

'You didn't offer to have coffee with *me*!' said Philippa, petulantly.

'Don't sound so disappointed—he didn't offer me any either. I had to *ask*!' Jo said dryly. 'Actually we weren't hitting it off at all well when you arrived.'

'We do seem to disagree violently!' Marsh drawled, and met Jo's green eyes briefly.

'How strange! I'm always at ease with him!' Philippa maintained, watching them both closely. 'We were discussing things to do to entertain you and the children.'

'How kind!'

'Do you ride?' Philippa asked loftily. 'Everyone rides!'

'I did try once, but I was more off than on,' Jo admitted.

Marsh gave a soft amused laugh. 'Can't you really?'

'It would be stupid to deny it. You'll soon see!'

'How extraordinary!' drawled Philippa, the expert horsewoman. 'How very odd!'

'One usually saves up for a car in the city!'

'But surely as a part-time occupation?'

'I rarely have the time to pursue such things.'

'Jo is thinking of redecorating Malakai,' Marsh offered, rather slyly, Jo thought.

This might have been a red flag to a bull. Philippa let both elbows fall forward on the table while her lacy neckline plunged alarmingly. 'Don't try it!' she snapped. 'Don't even move a stick of furniture!'

'Not until I inspect the place more thoroughly,' Jo said camly. 'I'm jam-packed with ideas!'

'I'll bet!' Philippa seconded as though she suddenly found Jo smarter than she had given her credit for. 'You don't really want anything changed, do you, Marsh? I mean, you couldn't bear it, could you? Your family home!'

'It could do with a little updating!' Marsh smiled at her and Jo had to admit that as a smile it was really something.

'But, darling,' she looked furiously agitated, 'surely you should leave that to your future wife? Everybody knows most women want to decorate their own home!'

'As a matter of fact,' Jo assured her, 'a lot of them prefer to leave it to those that know best!'

'And you do?'

'I've got certificates to prove it.'

'I'd certainly like to look at them!' Philippa replied smartly. 'I gather you don't approve of Mrs McConnell's taste? Marsh's mother, I mean!'

'I know Mrs McConnell approves of mine,' said Jo. 'Apparently Marsh is trying to tease you. What we were actually talking about was redoing the kitchen.'

'Ellen might have something to say about that,' Philippa persisted. 'After all, this is her domain!'

'And I know she's going to be happy with my plans,' Jo said very confidently. 'After all, such a marvellous cook takes pride in her kitchen and I'm going to make it easier for her to work in it.'

'Well, really!' Philippa tried a smile. 'I'm none too sure now of your real position—nanny or decorator!'

'He'll have to pay me for the latter,' Jo said laconically. 'And I'm not cheap!'

'I don't think there can be any doubt that you're a fast worker!' Philippa exchanged a complicated look with Marsh.

'Be that as it may, I'm taking myself off now,' said Jo, getting up. 'Thanks for the coffee, Marsh!'

'I spent a little time making toast as well!' He came gracefully to his feet, topping Jo by many inches.

'Thanks for that too!' Her mouth twisted and there was some feeling between them impossible to define—a guarded liking, for all their clashes.

'See you in the morning, Philippa!' she smiled at the younger girl whose countenance showed a remarkable lack of acceptance of her very presence, but Philippa held up her glowing auburn head to say:

'Yes, I'm in no hurry to get away. I may be able to give you a few pointers on how to stay on a horse! I'm sure Marsh has some sympathetic old nag somewhere on the property.'

'Neither of you put yourselves out on my account. As far as I'm concerned if I can't do it on my own two legs I'll take the car. There can't be many places a four-wheel-drive can't go!'

'Don't be difficult!' Marsh murmured. 'I'll show you. You'll be safe with me.'

Jo nodded her head, not evading the brilliant black gaze. Amazingly she believed him. She shivered, remembering the brush of his lips against her skin, then she raised her hand briefly in salutation and went back along the corridor up the stairway to her room. Her head was swimming a little, but never unpleasantly. In this strange new environment she was coping quite well.

CHAPTER FIVE

NEXT morning Jo left Paddy comfortably sleeping and went down to breakfast accompanied by Jenny. The night had passed without incident and Jo found herself unexpectedly refreshed. Morning in the Outback was miraculous; to be awakened by vigorous bird song, an impromptu performance that was overwhelmingly beautiful, the stream of air through the french doors, pure and invigorating, deliciously dry, an aromatic blend of gum trees, boronia and the good earth. She had to get up and explore at all costs. Jenny too had been lying awake entranced by the feathered orchestra, smiling at Jo across her small brother's sleeping form, so quietly they had dressed and gone downstairs.

Philippa was already seated at the table in the breakfast room, which housed a splendid collection of carved English oak pieces. Her bright head was clearly defined against the streaming bands of golden sunlight that struck through the window wall, but her hard topaz eyes within their spiky fringe of lashes suggested she wasn't all that pleased to have company.

'Good morning!' she said, very much the lady of the house.

Jo and Jenny roused themselves to respond pleasantly and sat down at the enormous table.

'Ellen will be in presently,' Philippa informed them. 'Sleep well?'

'Yes, thank you,' Jo answered for both of them. 'We left Paddy to wake up in his own good time. He seems to be over whatever it was.'

'Perhaps you didn't feed him right!' Philippa suggested, harking back.

'I'm dying to explore!' Jenny said rapturously gazing out at the bush.

Philippa fairly frowned. 'Some areas of the house will be out of bounds!'

Jo looked up, surprised. 'Marsh said nothing about that. Where is he?'

Philippa gave a cool little laugh, her eyes bright with malice. 'You won't find Marsh sitting about idly this time of the morning. He's been up and about for hours. You *have* noticed the house is a show place. It has an extensive collection of antiques and valuable family heirlooms. Naturally children aren't encouraged to run through it!'

Jenny threw up her fair head so fast her thick plait swung. 'We have antiques at home!' she said, incensed and quite out of harmony with the arrogant Philippa, who ignored her.

'Yes, it's quite a museum one way and another. You *do* see what I mean?'

'I'm responsible for the children,' Jo returned quietly. 'Depend on me to keep them out of trouble. Actually they've been brought up to revere beautiful things. Their father is an architect.'

'Even so, they're *children*!' Philippa flashed back with a tiny smile.

Jo swallowed, but was prevented from answering as two little aboriginal children wandered into the room, standing hand in hand just inside the door. They looked as enchanting a pair as one could wish to see, so totally identical they had to be twins, although they were in fact boy and girl disguised in the unisex T-shirt and shorts. Philippa glanced about sharply, blinked her eyes as though to clear them of an unwelcome vision, then gave a controlled clap of her hands.

'*Shoo!*'

'Oh really, they're not chickens!' Jenny, greatly taken, danced out of her chair and up to the pair. 'Aren't you gorgeous? Like the little tintookies that run about the sandhills at night!' The children stood their ground, looking up at her, their great liquid eyes filling their round shiny faces. Jenny bent and patted each one lovingly on the head exactly as if they were puppies. 'Hello there. I'm Jenny and that's Jo.'

'You'll have to wash your hands if you're having breakfast!' Philippa warned with a virulent brand of hygiene.

Jenny rounded on her, looking curiously shocked, but was quelled by the look in Jo's green eyes. 'Who are they?' she asked after a minute.

'Nara's brats!' Philippa said casually, finishing off the last mouthful of bacon. 'Unwelcome too. Some white man left her stranded on the fringe of the desert. Marsh found them and brought them in. All three of them were starving. Nothing strange about that.'

'How shocking!' exclaimed Jo.

'Little half-castes like Nara wander all round the place,' Philippa continued with a chilling lack of humanity. 'She feels she's found a place here.'

'I certainly hope so,' said Jo fervently. 'She's little more than a child herself.'

'Compared to you and me she's a thousand years old!' Philippa said derisively.

'And I wouldn't like her lot!' Jo answered quietly. 'The children are beautiful and they look very healthy.'

'You should have seen them when they arrived—covered in sores, all their bones sticking out. Jenny, do come away!' Philippa broke off sharply. 'They have no business to be in here. I'll speak to Nara. Unlike most of her people, she doesn't know her place.'

There was a short silence and Jo shifted restlessly in her chair. 'I'd better go through and see Ellen.'

'It's all right, I'm here now.' In a few seconds Ellen's calm drawl was translated into her sturdy reality. She was carrying two covered entrée dishes and she put them down on the sideboard before turning to Jo and the children. 'Well now, how's everyone this morning? I see you've met the twins.'

'What are their names?' Jenny flashed Ellen a quick, smiling look.

'Lula and Laurie, that's what we call them. Engaging little mites, aren't they?'

'I don't particularly like them in the dining room!' Philippa pointed out curtly.

Ellen turned to look at her in a startled way then her motherly face flushed. 'I didn't realise,' she said quietly, and put both her work-worn hands on the twins' shoulders, turning them about. 'Go on, children, go back to the kitchen. It isn't like Nara to let them get away from her. They must have wandered in when we weren't looking.'

'I'm glad they did!' Jo uncoiled herself and walked over to the oak sideboard. 'They're extraordinarily attractive!' She lifted the lids of the dishes and sniffed appreciatively. 'Nothing wrong with my appetite this morning. This looks delicious, Ellen. I like a good breakfast.'

Ellen turned to her with obvious relief, relaxed by Jo's natural manner and her beautiful bright appearance. 'I looked in on young Paddy this morning,' she said. 'He was sleeping peacefully.'

'Yes. If only he comes down and has a good breakfast we'll know he's all right!'

'I've just been telling Ellen your plans for renovating her kitchen,' Philippa said clearly, her motive apparent.

Jo, busy spooning cereal and peaches into Jenny's dish, looked up, rueful and embarrassed. 'You might have let *me* do that!'

Ellen touched her arm as if to say, That's all right. 'Tell me all about it after breakfast. I can do with all the help I can get.'

Jo looked into her pleasant, lined face seeking some

sign of injured feelings. 'It's just that I've studied these things, Ellen. Please don't think I'm interfering. Such a very large area makes for a good deal of extra work, and I would like to show you what can be achieved to suit you better.'

'Then tell me when I've got a free minute,' Ellen suggested. 'I'll be all ears. Now sit down and have your breakfast while it's nice and hot. Anything else you want, just ring.'

'I'll have some fresh tea!' Philippa put in a little shortly.

'Well now, I'll go and get it. There's coffee for you, Jo. I remembered you like it!'

Jo gave her irresistible smile. 'Thanks, Ellen. I'm longing to look around the place.'

Ellen glanced down at the old-fashioned watch pinned to her uniform front. 'We won't see Marsh until lunch time, but you'll find plenty to occupy you. You could take morning tea down to the Ten Mile if you like.'

Very speakingly Philippa placed her empty tea cup down on its saucer and Ellen glanced about, dashed, then made off at speed.

'Really, Ellen gets slower and slower!' Philippa drawled.

'Maybe she's overworked,' Jo suggested.

'I've come to a different conclusion myself. She's simply getting older!'

Jo could feel herself getting angry. 'Marsh seems very fond of her,' she pointed out rather helplessly against Philippa's distinctly cold attitude.

'You're telling me! The old retainer bit. I bet he's going to pension her off nicely!' Philippa gave that tiny little smile again. 'I'm only biding my time before working on his staffing arrangements.'

'Oh, I'm sure you'll do a marvellous job!'

Philippa accepted this as a compliment. 'Tell me, what

do you intend to do with the children all day?' she asked.

Carefully Jo buttered her toast. 'Whatever we feel like. Routine leassons so they won't fall too far behind in their school work, then anything we think of. This is a wonderful new world!'

'I can imagine *you* might regard it as such!' She said dryly.

'Why not?' Jo levelled a very direct glance. 'I'm city bred. This is all new to me.'

'I can't think you're particularly well suited to it,' shrugged Philippa. 'It's a decided disadvantage not to be able to ride.'

Jo had a momentary sensation of nausea. 'I don't think it matters at all. Anyway, Marsh seems very keen on making it easy for me. I imagine he's a wonderful teacher!'

'And I wouldn't bother him if I were you,' said Philippa, breathing more deeply.

'But I'm not you!' Jo returned quietly. 'And I don't particularly want to be!'

Philippa gave a mirthless crow of laughter. 'Thank you. Just so long as we know where we are!'

Jenny put her spoon down and said in a half-strangled voice, 'I don't think I want this!'

'Oh, for heaven's sake, *eat* it!' Philippa spat out impatiently. 'We can't have both of you sick.' She wiped her mouth delicately and threw down her napkin. 'I don't think I'll bother with that tea. I'm going to ride out and join Marsh. Tell Ellen when she finally gets here.'

'I'll tell her now!' Jenny offered, and jumped up from the table, fleeing the room.

Jo was suddenly furiously angry. She didn't even hesitate to speak her mind. 'Please don't speak so sharply to Jenny!' she said formally. 'You seem to be going out of your way to upset her!'

'Pity!' Philippa returned fatuously. She stood up and

drew away from the table, giving Jo a look of utter
detestation.

'Marsh is very fond of them,' Jo added sternly. 'He
invited them here.'

'Oh?' The rosebud mouth curled. 'And you're going to
be the nasty tattle-tale?'

Jo looked up at the petite curvy shape wearing the
same T-shirt and tight jeans as yesterday. 'Why should I
want to upset such a beautiful relationship? You just
have to look out for *me*!'

Philippa sneered, 'Quite the tigress, aren't you?'

'It's my job!'

'Substitute mother? You're no chicken either!'

'You'll have to be fairly quick yourself. Unless I'm
mistaken you're only about eighteen months younger.'

'But I'm very nearly there!' Philippa pointed out
smilingly. 'With all due respect, Miss Adams, we didn't
need you here, yet you've "happened" to make yourself
part of the household. It's a bit tricky, to say the least.
To put it plainly, it doesn't suit me!'

'What a mercy you can't tell me to go!'

'No,' Philippa returned with that same acid smile, 'I
can't very easily do that, but I can warn you you'll be
making a big mistake, if you try to cause trouble between Marsh and me.'

'You speak as though you're inseparable!'

'Practically. We have a different way of life out here,
Miss Adams. Our property adjoins Malakai on the north-
east border. One day Summerfield will be mine. Get the
drift?'

'Oh, it's very clearly in focus!' said Jo, torn between
fury and amusement. 'Why get so uptight about me?'

'Because I think I'm dealing with a conniving
woman!' said Philippa, her topaz eyes narrowing.

'Well,' Jo returned with dignity, 'is there another
kind?'

Philippa took a moment to digest this and her pale

skin flushed. 'You joke, Miss Adams, but I'm deadly serious. You'll take a great deal of the pressure off yourself if you remember Marsh is *mine*!'

'If you say so!' Jo bent her head in quick deference. 'May I suggest you go out and find him? You're ruining my appetite!'

'I'm going!' Philippa said tightly. 'It's a shame to waste yourself out here. You're so witty and all!'

'I like you too, incidentally,' returned Jo.

'That's quite all right with me. Four weeks passes quickly.' Philippa bent over, picked up her wide-brimmed hat and went out.

In another minute Jenny returned and patted Jo very kindly on the shoulder. 'Isn't she awful?' she said.

'I'm sure deep down, she's quite nice!' Jo said wryly.

'I think she makes Ellen feel a failure!'

'She does have a deflationary effect, yes,' Jo conceded. 'Sit down, darling, and finish your breakfast. What would you like now?'

'Some scrambled egg, please.' Jenny slipped back on to her chair. 'I'm going to play with the twins for a little while. Is that all right?'

'Of course. It will give me an opportunity to attend to Paddy. Once we've settled in we'll start lessons for an hour in the morning, then again in the afternoon. The last thing we want is to have you fall behind in your school work!'

'Oh, that doesn't matter!' Jenny said carelessly. 'I'm pretty well on top of everything. Daddy told me to get out and enjoy myself. I do hope that's what *they're* doing!' Anxious grey eyes looked into Jo's, seeking confirmation.

Jo's irritations with Philippa fell away from her. 'Don't worry, darling,' she said lightly, 'they'll have lots and lots of wonders stored up to tell us about. Eat up now. Ellen wants us to take morning tea down to the Ten Mile, wherever that may be.'

Jenny gave a lighthearted peal of laughter, forking into the fluffy pile of scrambled egg. 'Oh, I should say ten miles away at the least. Do you think Paddy will be well enough to come?'

'In a few minutes we'll see. I've an idea we're going to have lots of adventures ourselves!'

Jo came down on the crossing with a warm glow of achievement on her face. Navigation wasn't her strong point, as she was endowed with the usual feminine capacity for misreading turn-offs, but that surely was the crossing, with only a few inches of water gurgling around the creek stones before racing away on either side to the deep billabongs.

The trip out from the homestead had been full of wondrous sights; the great vault of the sky shimmering above them, the blue dancing mirage, the grassy savannah strewn with paper-like daisies, grazing cattle, the great stands of trees, the distant loop of the river, the wide open spaces, hundreds and hundreds of miles of wide open country, the flocks of corellas that cloaked the branches of the river gums, the phenomenon of the Outback, the undulating flights of budgerigars, the tiny shell green parrots as they took dominion of the sky. It was a special happiness, nature, and it had great healing power, lightening Jo's heart so she could do little but accept her life as it was and even join with the children in singing about it. It was that kind of a morning.

Timber planks spanned the narrow creek crossing and she lined up the utility carefully. She had no real worry. She was an experienced driver and she *had* found the way. Only a few miles beyond was the Ten Mile, the mustering camp, and the men were waiting.

Paddy looked up into her face seeking an answer to his curiosity. 'What's that over there?' he asked.

'Where?' Only Jenny turned her head. Jo didn't want to be distracted at that time.

'It looked like a dog. It was *huge*!' Paddy's voice suggested King Kong proportions.

'It might have been a dingo!' said Jenny, peering along the tree-lined creek bed.

'It looked more like a wolf!'

'I can't see anything!' Jenny said, suddenly suspicious.

Jo still didn't bother to look. They were on to the planks now and Paddy suddenly grabbed her arm in alarm. 'Oh, please, Aunty Jo! It's there!'

Distracted, she lost control of the wheel. The utility tilted and the front offside wheel left the plank and sank in the sand. 'Just my luck!' she wailed with self-pity.

'Didn't you see it?' Paddy insisted.

'Paddy dear!' Jo tried to remain calm. 'I suppose there are always a few dingoes about.'

'It wasn't a dingo, Aunty Jo. It was the horriblest dog I've ever seen—a blue-grey-black thing. I'm going to tell Uncle Marsh!'

'If we ever get to see him!' Jo muttered grimly. She was roaring the engine and the wheels were spinning uselessly. She kept at it, to no avail. They were bogged; she was certain of that. The children stared at her, trying to read her mind.

'Can we get out?' they asked.

'Not if there's that big dog out here. Are you certain you saw it?'

'What a nuisance you are, Paddy!' Jenny said wrathfully.

Paddy's blue eyes filled with tears. 'I *told* you I saw it. Why don't we go and have a look?'

'Not on your life. It might decide to make a meal of us!' As soon as she said it Jo regretted it, for the children looked about them too carefully.

'I tell you what!' she said brightly, and turned the engine off. 'I'll get out and have a look at the damage. I've a feeling explanations are going to be useless. Uncle

Marsh will probably have to pull us out.'

'It was Paddy's fault!' Jenny complained, looking askance at the small uncomfortable bundle at her side.

'It wasn't anyone's fault!' Jo said firmly. 'Maybe the big dog's. Suppose we give it a name?'

'How about Crocker?' Jenny suggested.

'Why Crocker?'

'Isn't there someone called Mad Dog Crocker?'

'I'm not altogether sure.' Jo slipped off her sandals and turned up the hems of her cotton slacks. 'Just sit here, and don't touch anything.' She opened the door and stood down on the creek bed. The water was astonishingly cold. It even shocked the soles of her feet and the pebbles dug into her tender toes. She picked her way gingerly around the bonnet of the utility and inspected the partly submerged wheel. 'Oh dear, oh dear! Just as we were doing so nicely!'

Jenny put her head out of the window and screeched, 'Jo!'

The eerie fright in her voice was apparent, and Jo straightened up at once and looked over her shoulder to see what had startled the child. On the opposite bank, coming down through the trees, was a lone wild dog of such height and weight Jo could feel herself break out in a sweat of paralysis.

'Good grief!' she gasped.

'Get back in the car!' shouted Jenny with great presence of mind.

The dog was looking right at them, eyes gleaming, tongue lolling. It was a mixture of strains, staghound, cattle dog, Alsatian, dingo—a dangerous relic of the old days when pastoralists had imported deerhounds and staghounds to run down a number of things: convicts, wild aboriginals, kangaroos, foxes, dingoes. Some of them had been crossed with greyhounds and bloodhounds to produce the powerful Kangaroo dogs. This one Jo thought of as Crocker was a mixture of colouring;

black and tan on the head, blue-grey on the haunches, gold undermarkings. From its watching stillness it wasn't afraid of humans. Jo picked up a stone and hurled it, but it fell short of its purpose, for the wild dog circled a fallen stump, then padded purposefully into the water.

That was enough for Jo. She turned about and made a rush for the car, clambered in and banged the door.

'Press the lock down!' she ordered Jenny.

'I already have. Now I'm going to wind up the window!'

Jo did the same, then pressed down hard on the horn as some effective means of combating the dog's menace. Paddy was trembling a little, staring intently, and Jo slipped her arm around him while continuing to press down hard on the horn. 'Uncle Marsh will hear us, and it can't get inside the car!'

'I've never seen a wild dog before!' he said, torn between fright and excitement. 'Why is it here?'

'Don't ask me. Perhaps it wants a drink of water.'

'Why did it have to choose here?'

Jo said nothing, her hand cupping his small shoulder. Along the twisted track on the other side of the creek two riders were approaching. When they glanced away from the welcome whirl of dust and back to the dog again, it had disappeared.

'It's gone!' Jenny dared to breathe. 'I'll wind down the window. It's so hot!'

'The horses must have frightened it,' said Jo.

In another minute Marsh rode into the creek coming up alongside Jo's side of the utility and bending sideways in the saddle and lightly holding the reins. 'Well, if we're going to starve we might as well die laughing!' he drawled.

'It could have happened to anybody!' said Jo, meeting his black eyes beneath the cream brim of his hat. There were little silver sparks of light in the centre of darkness.

'Couldn't you have made a damper of something?' she asked flippantly. 'I mean, it's a tradition in the bush, isn't it? Damper and billy tea!'

'But then we were expecting Ellen's scones!'

'I'm sorry. What else can I say?'

'How about the inevitable? You're a lousy driver!'

Philippa, astride a beautiful palomino, remained on the bank looking scornful, an expression that suited her well. Anyone who couldn't negotiate a simple creek crossing had no business driving station property, she seemed to say.

Marsh circled the utility, then rode back alongside. 'It shouldn't be too difficult getting you out,' he commented.

'I've tried!' Jo said sweetly.

His expression spoke volumes. 'Maybe you used the wrong method.'

'Listen, Uncle Marsh, there was this great big wolf!' Paddy broke in excitedly.

'Not around here!' Marsh threw him an indulgent glance.

'Be that as it may, I threw a stone at it!' said Jo.

He bent his head sharply. 'What are you talking about?'

'It's gone now, but there was some kind of hound over there,' she told him.

He looked away across the stream, then walked his horse towards Philippa. After a few moments' conversation she headed the palomino into the crossing to draw alongside Jo. 'You ought to take a few lessons in handling a ute,' she said in a low, maddening tone.

'What in the world are you talking about? This is a small thing, surely?'

The topaz eyes glittered. 'The men are waiting for smoko. They work extremely hard and it's hot, thirsty work.'

'Then why don't you take it to them?' Jo suggested.

'Exactly why I'm here. If you wouldn't mind tying the

tablecloth around whatever Ellen has prepared.'

Jo got out of the utility again. She went around to the back, unclipped the canvas, spread the tablecloth and tipped the trayful of scones on to it, drawing up the edges and knotting them. She made sure there was no gaping hole, then she lifted the warm fragrant bundle and handed it up to Philippa, who was standing her horse unnecessarily close.

Philippa accepted it without a word and made back across the creek, nodding at Marsh, then heading off into the silent bush. Marsh by this time had tethered the big bay he had been riding and waded into the creek, looking with faint amusement at Jo's slacks. One leg was still rolled up, but the other had come down and the hem was soaking wet. 'Why don't you just stand out of the way?'

'It's in pretty deep.'

'How did this breathless incident occur?' he asked.

Jo shrugged. 'Just one of those things!'

'I suppose you can't have everything!' he said lazily. He climbed into the utility, said something to the children that made them laugh, then he turned on the engine. It fired immediately and the vehicle began to move.

It hadn't crossed Jo's mind to reverse and now she wondered, mortified, why she hadn't. Marsh simply shunted the vehicle back and forth until gradually the wheel inched up on to the plank again. The next minute it rolled up on to the other side and dry land. The children cheered and she considered she had been taught Lesson One. It would never have happened without Crocker. By the time she waded across they were all standing outside the utility and Paddy was pointing out the exact place the wild dog had come down on the creek.

Marsh's face was expressionless. 'Then we'll be able to pick up its tracks.'

'It may still be around!' said Jo, not relaxing her stand of protecting the children.

'No. It will have moved off now. But it won't escape. We haven't had a case of a dingo moving so close in.'

'It wasn't a dingo. It was a mixture of half a dozen strains so far as I could tell—a shaggy-haired wolf dog with a lot of Alsatian in it.'

He looked at her closely, his dark eyes scanning her face. 'You're quite sure?'

'It was just as I've described!'

'Then God knows how it's come this far. There have been reports, but that was months ago. It will be necessary to kill it. It could savage the calves. You go ahead. Follow the track through the trees.'

'Will you be all right?' she queried.

He pushed his slouch hat back on his head, running a hand through the crisp wave at his temple. He looked vital and mocking and as Aunt Elizabeth had once said, far from ordinary. 'Are you worried?' he drawled.

'To my moderate surprise, yes!'

'That's what I get for rescuing you.' He glanced at the children and grinned, 'Ungrateful, isn't she?'

'I suppose I'd better say thank you,' said Jo stiffly.

'You might have to say it over and over before the month's out!'

'Actually it was Paddy's fault!' Jenny said fairly. 'He grabbed at Jo's arm.'

'Anyway, he's his old self this morning, that's the main thing,' answered Marsh. 'Take the children along, Jo, and let them have morning tea with the men. They'll enjoy it.'

'And you?'

'I'll join you when I can.'

She looked around at this wild, untamed world, but she couldn't very well prevent him from doing what he had to. 'All right, then. Take care!'

'I did explain to you the way to go?' he called after her dryly.

'I'll find it!'

She ushered the children into the utility, then turned

about to look at him. There was a strength and a
vibrancy about him, an easy casualness, that provoked
her. She had never really taken much notice of a man's
physique before, but she was very conscious that he was
superbly built; wide-shouldered, narrow-waisted, lean-
hipped, the ripple of whipcord muscles just beneath the
smooth, darkly-tanned skin. The silver glint of a medal-
lion caught the sunlight. She wondered why he wore it,
not knowing that his mother, reared a Catholic, had
placed it around his neck as a protection after his father
had been killed, insisting he wear it always. She didn't
realise she was staring, but she had to come out of her
trance as he swept off his hat, bringing it across his body
in a theatrical bow. Even at that distance the air fairly
crackled with electricity.

Jo tossed her head, flushing; and got into the utility,
then she started up the engine and took off along the
track with a dazzling burst of speed. She was in a
strange state of mind, taut with a kind of excited energy.
Contact with Marsh McConnell was proving distracting.
He was a hard man to ignore. He looked magnificent on
a horse and his hair in the sunlight had the polished
gleam of ebony. She was startled she had noticed so
much, and the memory remained.

Afterwards Jo was to wonder where the days went. They
seemed to fly past on wings and they were quite outside
her normal experience. Always a night owl, she now
found herself rising with the birds, if only because the
children did and retiring early to meet the physical
demands of the next day. It took her less than a week to
establish beyond any possible doubt that Paddy was
indeed accident-prone, and as she said wryly to Ellen as
she fished him out of the ornamental pond 'it gave her
something to shoot for' keeping him on his feet. Paddy
seemed to go through the day creating his own obstacle
courses, but he was so lovable, so sunny-natured that

even Nara didn't blame him when he let her pet snake escape.

Every morning after breakfast Marsh supervised her riding lesson and Jo, to her mounting pleasure and confidence, took to it naturally, though it would be many a long day before she became an expert like Philippa, who seemed to call in every other day on the radio transceiver. Lessons took up another hour, and the children were fascinated by the School of the Air broadcasts, listening far more intently, Jo suspected, than they ever did at their expensive private schools. After that they were free to cram in experiences as though they had to fit everything in in a few short weeks. With Nara as guide they went on nature studies and walks while she threaded the hours with the beautifully imaginative legends and the secrets and mysteries of her mother's people. When they picnicked or went swimming at any one of the tree-lined waterholes the twins came too, increasing the older children's pleasure, for like their mother the twins had some attraction impossible to ignore. Other days they watched the men mustering and cutting cattle, though tender-hearted Paddy didn't like the branding or the smell, but an impromptu meal over the camp fire always revived him, and the novelty of a mug of milked-down billy tea.

So far they hadn't slept out under the stars, but Uncle Marsh had promised and the children were determined to keep him to it. The trip into the silent hill country to see the sacred places and inspect the cave drawings he had ruled out until he could accompany them, and after the spring showers, he said, he would take them all out to the desert fringe to see the unending vistas of wild-flowers and the red pyramids of the sandhills. These experiences were invaluable and were treated as an important part of their education.

For the past few days the men were working closer in to the compound, but so far Crocker the wild dog had

eluded capture. No stock losses were reported and no
further sightings made. The dog could be anywhere on
the vast property, and Marsh's instructions were to
shoot it on sight. Wild dogs and feral cats created their
own menace, and it was thought the staghound had gone
deeper into the bush. The seasons had been good, so it
couldn't have been short of food. Curiosity alone had led
it in so close to camp.

With her days so full of activity in the pure fresh air
Jo found herself sleeping deeply and dreamlessly at
night. Even her subconscious refused to draw on her
treasured memories of Blair. She saw now that her
complete change of environment had come as a great
blessing, and coping with the children, especially Paddy,
left little time for moping or introspection. Blair be-
longed to Julie by choice. She would have to keep on
saying 'No!' to his memory until it too became habit.
Maybe her lonely childhood had made her cling to him
to the point of obsession. Little did she realise she was
soon to be tested when she was far from prepared for
it.

That particular morning all three of them were sitting
on the white-railed fence watching Ned, the station horse
breaker and something of a legend, 'talking' to one of
the brumbies. Ned was an old part-aboriginal bushman
and he had a considerable gift for entertaining his audi-
ence. Quite a few of the men had sauntered up to watch
and Marsh too joined them for a moment, speaking
briefly to Jo:

'I've some news for you.'

'Oh, what?' She turned to smile at him.

The breeze caught at her hair and he put out a hand to
tuck a strand away from her face. 'My mother and Julie
are flying in for a few days. Julie wants to know can she
bring her fiancé.'

Jo stared at him and her heart began to hammer.
'*What* did you say?' Her voice rose so sharply Paddy

rocked in astonishment and Marsh caught him round the waist and held him steady.

'Look at that now!' he digressed for the children's benefit, temporarily ignoring Jo or giving her time to get over her shock. 'This is what we call horse psychology. It replaces the force you've seen. Ned is very successful at this—in fact he's the finest horse-breaker in this part of the world. You've seen both methods of breaking now. This one, if one has the gift for it, is vastly superior. Ned can ride anything in less than an hour. That's bareback and a wild horse from the range, and he can make any horse acceptable for normal stock work in a couple of days.'

'But he's just talking to them, Uncle Marsh!' Jenny swung her face around. It had tanned to an entrancing light gold and she looked happier and better looking than she had done only a short week before.

'And that's how he does it!' Marsh explained. 'It's a very gentle art. I practice it myself. In fact I'll show you tomorrow how I gentle a horse. I want to talk to Aunty Jo now.' He glanced back over his shoulder and called to Barney, who came up at a fast trot. 'Look after the children, will you, Barney? I have some news for Miss Jo!'

'Will do, Boss!' Barney grinned, and climbed nimbly on to the fence. Both children, having spent some time following him around, flashed a smile. They liked him and he had their full confidence, but evidently Paddy didn't have Barney's, for his wiry arm stayed protectively at the little boy's back.

Marsh looked back at Jo, registering the shock in her eyes. His own face tightened into something like formidability and he put up a hand to help her down, then led her some little distance away to the shade of the gums. 'No doubt you'll tell me in your own good time!' she started out unfairly.

'Yes, the unforgettable Blair!' he picked up the story,

paying her out by ignoring her wretchedness. 'Do you want him to come?'

'Why would Julie want to bring him here?' she demanded, genuinely puzzled.

'Believe it or not, she wants to be married from here. Surely you realised I was to give her away?'

'You do what you think best!' she said bitterly, and turned away.

'I'd have staked my life you were forgetting him,' said Marsh.

'I didn't expect him to follow me out here!'

'Turn around!' he said curtly. 'If it's going to affect you so badly I'll say no.'

Vaguely she was aware that he had turned her and was holding her by the shoulders. 'I've no idea why you want to help me,' she said flatly.

'I admire the way you're looking after the children,' he said offhandedly. 'It's Aunty Jo this, and Aunty Jo that. Even Ellen has taken to it these days. I believe my nose is out of joint. I used to be their most attractive relation.'

'I'm nothing compared to you!' she said absentmindedly. 'When are they coming?'

'Brace yourself, dear girl!' He gave a very elegant shrug. 'The day after tomorrow—if you give the O.K. Well?'

Jo glanced up to find he was watching her closely like a cat watches a mouse, ready to pounce.

'It seems to me you're enjoying this!' she said crossly.

'Why shouldn't I?' he asked shortly. 'You're looking particularly delectable these days.'

As usual she ignored his compliments and he laughed gently, transferring his hands into his pockets. 'Maybe his presence will resolve a few things.'

Jo's spirits were visibly waning. 'I'll probably have nightmares tonight!' she warned.

'Would you like me to call in on you?' he asked suavely.

'If you did you'd get knocked back!'

'Come now!' His brilliant eyes narrowed. 'You can trust me. As it stands now I've only kissed you the once!'

'Twice!' she corrected sharply, and coloured despite herself.

Marsh made a soft jeering noise in his throat. 'Nothing more than a chaste peck. That simply doesn't count, but it's nice to know you remembered.'

Her green eyes gave him the speaking glance she reserved for him, glowing with exasperated challenge. She even had to admit that she revelled in their odd clashes, and it was surely strange. Like the children's, her skin had turned to gold and she looked anything but a woman suffering a heavy black burden of rejection. Her eyes, hair and skin gleamed with health and she looked beautifully slender and relaxed in her loose cotton shirt and tan-gold slacks.

'Maybe I'm treating you with too much delicacy,' Marsh said dryly. 'After all, you're not a young girl!'

'And I'm not a thousand either!' she cried, stung by the taunt.

He laughed again and she had to endure it, for he looked treacherously vital and masculine and he had really, when it was all said and done, carried her off. 'Let's call a truce!' he said lightly. 'Come riding with me this afternoon. Nara can look after the kids for an hour or so. They can do a bit of painting in the garden and they like to play with the twins.'

'I don't know!' Something told her to hesitate. He was really a very tempestuous man, for all the smooth façade. Too sharp for her palate—unique in a way. There was too much stir and challenge about him. He made her think, and she didn't want to. He could also make her *feel*, she had discovered to her horror, and all too simply. He had to be treated with the utmost caution.

'I suppose there's no escape, is there?' she said, look-ing poignant and passionate all at once.

'What from—me?' he grinned.

'From life.'

'Why complain? You're doing all right. Now, are you coming or not? I'm a busy man.'

'Indeed you are!' she agreed admiringly. 'It's come as an eye-opener to see exactly how hard you do work.'

'Don't tell me you thought I was useless?' he said acidly. 'By the way, Ellen was having a bit of trouble interpreting your drawings. The thing over her head. What was that supposed to be?'

Jo frowned, caught up in the tricks of her trade again. 'That's a utensil rack. We'll have it especially made— everything arranged for her just where it's the most convenient.'

'Tell her!' he said dryly. 'She thought it was a bit of nonsense like an outsized halo!'

'She deserves one, and she's enjoying the thought of the changes, don't you worry,' Jo retorted. 'She spends so much time in the kitchen I'm going to make it the show place of the South-West for her.'

'We're all anticipating that!' Marsh said blandly. 'I hope Leighton doesn't have any ideas!'

'Then consider, is it wise to let him come?' she answered sharply, not liking the expression on his face. McConnell, the hunter.

'Depend on it, he'll be right under my nose. So will you!'

'The best laid plans go astray!' she said perversely.

'You don't worry me, green eyes,' he drawled. 'You don't even know yourself yet. I'll get one of the boys to saddle up Honey for you. We'll start out after lunch.'

'You're the boss!'

'I'm also the teacher. You're coming along fine!'

They watered their horses at an aboriginal well and Jo

could see, in the distance, the rose red sandhills sharply outlined against the brilliant blue sky. The grassy, blue-flowered plains country resounded with bird calls, and they intended taking the narrow track down the acacia-lined gullies, the small lakes of clear water, to where the black swans nested and the brolgas performed their spectacular ballets. It was well over an hour since they had left the compound and the afternoon was passing in unusual accord; as though each of them had given a scared promise to call a halt on the verbal sparring that the interaction of their personalities seemed to demand.

Malakai was the kind of country that took hold of the heart. It could lead and direct lives, and Jo could see from the expression on Marsh's dominant dark face that an invisible, unbreakable cord bound him to it. The richness of bougainvillaea glowed even here, scarlet and pink and magenta, cassias spilled in warm golden showers and great greeny-grey stands of gums were dusted all over with powdery tassels of flowers. It was quite beyond human power to count the birds or the dazzling variety, and with so many lagoons they flapped and chattered and alighted all over, decorating the lignum clumps like huge brilliant flowers.

Marsh went out of his way to point out everything of interest; the huge area the Government geologists had assured him was rich in mineral depositis and which just happened to be on a prehistoric site; the fossilised rocks that held fast the skeletons of creatures from the great inland sea of prehistory; the places where he had found opal. They were travelling over country deep in native lore with many stone altars and sacred places for the getting of wisdom, hallowed ground, not understood by the white man. Apart from the birds there was a deep pervading silence like a Presence of Great Being hovering over his kingdom.

The peace was remarkable, and as Jo rode over the sloping grasslands she could feel it seeping right through to her heart. She had tried every tactic known to her to forget Blair, and Malakai seemed to be doing it for her. She hadn't thought it all through, and Marsh wasn't a man she could manage, but he was one with his land, a man trained to take over such an inheritance. Kangaroos and wallabies made shadowy movements in the long grass, but they didn't disturb anybody. Jo's only regret was that so far she hadn't seen one with a joey peeping out of its pouch.

The sun was well past its zenith when they rode down on the tree-shadowed swamp. Reeds and purple trumpet lilies fringed it round and up from the banks there were stands of wild flowering plum. Marsh took the horses' reins and tethered them to separate trees, then he joined Jo at the water's edge, looking downstream to where a black swan and her four fluffy white cygnets were gliding across the mirror-clear dark green stretch of water.

'How beautiful! I've never seen them in the wild!' she said.

'This is one of their favourite havens.'

For a time neither of them spoke, seemingly content with watching the regal progress of the mother swan across the water. The river coolibahs were heavy in blossom, their barks shining reddish-brown in the golden-green light, spirit trees and guardians of the waterways.

Jo lifted her arms above her head and sighed blissfully. 'I'm deliciously tired. I hope I didn't do anything to displease you?'

He swung back and stared straight at her. 'On the contrary, you're a natural in the saddle. With some solid practice you'd be good and you wouldn't find it quite so tiring. Why don't you rest a while and I'll go hunt up some of our own native orchids. They're scattered all over, but they're not that easy to find. The scent was clearer a few hundred yards back. They're beautiful and they keep a long time in water. They're supposed to possess some magic—Nara will tell you. You might be able to dry out the petals and crush them into a love potion.'

'Ever helpful?' she commented, unsure of him, for his dark face had hardened. 'I'll call out to you if I need you.'

'I'm not going far!' He gave a slight shrug. It seemed to be a characteristic and she realised she found it very attractive. 'You'll be able to see me all the way. I remember we found them here once in abundance. The perfume is not unlike the Queen of the Night.'

She listened with interest, holding her dark hair back from her face. 'Go and get it!' she smiled.

'And don't *you* run away!'

Jo smiled at him and he gave her a quick nod of approval, moving with his long lithe tread back along the track. It was amazing, but she could have gone instantly to sleep. Sunlight fell muted on her face and the fragrance of the lilies made her sigh with pleasure. She stretched out on the dry sandy bank, put her hands behind her head and closed her eyes. She'd been up so early, at first light. It was really fantastic the way Paddy selected that hour for waking her with a hand on her face. If that method failed he usually pulled her ear as if he was ringing in the New Year until finally she came awake and pretty much in control of things. She had always been a slow starter, but then she had never lived with children before.

It was wonderful, this place. Leaves rustled above her head, softly swishing like a native chant. She was hovering on the brink of sleep, all her senses surrendering to a delicious feeling of wellbeing. She would have to think of something to give Nara, a great big thank-you for the way she amused and stimulated the children and looked after them so well. A lovely little creature, Nara, with such an innocent beauty. How shockingly she had been treated! Marsh was really a very good man, and all the aboriginal people on his property looked to him as a natural leader. A lion of a man. Jo was coming to respect him herself.

When Marsh came back her dark lashes lay heavy and motionless on her cheeks. She looked rather fragile, far more vulnerable with her vivid, mobile face in repose, her thick shining hair fallen sideways and her beautiful mouth faintly parted. The silk shirt she wore lovingly followed the shape of her breasts and there was colour beneath her skin, a warm tinting of apricot giving depth to the golden tan. Marsh dropped down beside her, slid his arms beneath her and lifted her easily into his arms. His face if she could have seen it was that of a buccaneer—passionate, even violent, taking the woman he wanted.

She was dreaming as she hadn't done for weeks and she came out of it whispering languorously, even fretfully:

'Blair. Oh, Blair!'

Marsh reacted with a spurt of fury. His black eyes flashed, enough to send panic signals through any woman, and he tapped her cheek painfully.

'Wake up!' he said distinctly.

She opened her eyes, no longer abandoned to her dream, saw his face, and the melting settleness in her body was instantly transformed into a tense resistance. He didn't release her and the heat of his body was reaching her. On the bank beside him were a half a dozen overlapping bracts of beautiful orchids, white, cream and bronze-green, speckled with mauve. Their delicious spicy perfume flowered all around them.

'What's the matter?' Jo was shocked by Marsh's expression and the lightning flicker in his lustrous eyes, not understanding the rage that stirred in him.

He mimicked her spellbound tone and swept on harshly: 'I'm not Blair. But I'm sure I'll do!'

'And I can tell you that's unlikely!' Her dreamy look

was clearing miraculously. If this was his mood she wasn't going to submit without a struggle. 'What's this supposed to be?' She tried to wave her pinned arms to demonstrate. 'The seduction scene?'

'You've earned it!' he grated.

'Great! I always knew you had a devilish streak!'

'Grow up!' he said bluntly. 'And don't kick up a row. Your maidenly ways don't fit your face—or your shape!'

'So that's it?' she said wrathfully. 'I'm a fallen woman!'

'You should have made sure I wasn't looking. Such talent!'

'And you've been paying me out ever since!'

'You understand, don't you?' he demanded roughly, and now she found out he was violent too, because he was hurting her and not caring. Overhead a jewelled parrot flapped idly in the heat, then launched into flight seeking a quieter spot.

'Some day...' Jo threatened, gritting her teeth, then suddenly she whimpered, 'Oh, you brute!'

'I've known *worse* relationships!'

'Tell me why?'

He shook his head. 'I'm concerned about you, Josephine. How many men have made love to you?'

'On present average, one!' she returned acidly.

'That's what I thought. Leighton got in very early, almost like cradle-snatching, but you're a big girl now and you really need more experience. Otherwise how are you going to know when true love comes?'

'Why didn't you tell me it was going to be you?' she mocked him.

'I've been telling you all along!'

'And here I was thinking Philippa was the only answer!'

'I didn't say I didn't like her, but you're something else again.'

He was controlling her easily and she went limp, feigning a weak urgency. 'Please, Marsh. I feel giddy. I think I'm going to faint.'

'Oh no, you're not!' he said sharply. 'And don't you *Please, Marsh* me! You're going to open your mouth and whisper some of those endearments Leighton found it so easy to get out of you.'

'You don't know me very well, do you?' she hurled at him, 'and I'm starting to get mad!' Her body twisted against him, but it only served to arouse an unmistakable response. He put his hand over her mouth and held her thrown back against him till she quietened, then he took his hand away and crushed her mouth against his own, forcing it open and setting up a fantastic storm of feeling. Every nerve end was excitable, responsive, her dormant sensuality stirring too steeply to climb back. In some mysterious fashion she felt separated from her own mind, lost in his strength. He wasn't bothering to check this enravishment; his strong, beautiful hands cupped her breasts as though the shape and curve of a woman's body was exquisite, holding her to him almost slavishly though she wasn't even trying to get free. Though it was to agitate her afterwards, now she was wild and yielding, her skin overheated as though they were surrounded by a ring of fire.

'*Who am I?*' he asked against her mouth.

Jo couldn't answer—she didn't have the breath. Marsh was offering her a sensual experience that promised complete forgetfulness, an enchanted drug. It was typical of him, as overpowering as the flowering wilderness. She had believed what she told him. She loved Blair. She had been conditioned to love him, but a whole range of experience had been denied her. Marsh was remaking her with the confidence of a master, proving her body a liar, covering her face and her throat and her breast in kisses so bold, so natural, it was like another dimension. Something beyond sex was driving him as if he wanted control not only of her body but her heart and her mind.

The blood was roaring in her ears. She felt stirred to the point of exhausted tears, her fingers ridiculously entwined in the crisp curls of his hair, her own mouth lingering on his throat. It was as shocking as it was unexpected, but it was happening and she had lost all direction. Even the golden sunlight was dimming...

'Jo?' He was sitting above her, tilting her head forward.

'I'm all right!'

It took a few minutes for the weakness to pass and he looked searchingly down at her face. 'For heaven's sake! You've been kissed before!'

'You weren't kissing me,' she pointed out sourly. 'That was a ravishment!'

'Don't be ridiculous!' His black humour had passed, for he held up her chin indulgently. 'God knows what you'd claim if I did. I didn't hurt you either, though I came pretty close to it. It's really your own fault, falling asleep on the sand!'

From his eyes she knew that wasn't entirely the truth. 'I said something, didn't I?'

His white teeth snapped together. 'You were moaning very sweetly: "Blair, oh, Blair!"'

'And you went half mad with jealousy?'

'Don't kid yourself, lady. I resented his intrusion into my afternoon. What's with you, anyway? One minute you're trying to cut me down to size and the next you're fainting away in my arms!'

'I chose that way to make you let me go!' she retorted.

'Liar!' His magnificent black eyes were full of mockery. 'Do you even know what you want? You weren't pretending just then. I could have taken you at any time and you'd have let me. I know you, Josephine. You're a very fastidious girl, even old-fashioned, which I just happen to like. Can it be you've switched your affections?'

'No to all your questions!' she said shortly. 'It was such a lovely day. What a pity to spoil it!'

He gave that elegant dismissive shrug again. 'Have it your own way. I can see you're winded!'

'Oh go to the devil!'

Some sharp lively movement behind them halted all talk. The horses waiting up on the bank swung their heads up, nervously pawing the grass. Marsh took his arm away, half turning, his narrowed far-seeing eyes ranging over the trees and the lacing vines.

'What is it?' Jo was whispering, and suddenly everything seemed shadowy.

'God knows!' Marsh came up swiftly, bringing her with him, his dark face sharp in her mind. 'I'd better investigate. Something's spooking the horses!' His searching eyes found the outline of a sleek and heavy dingo bitch. He didn't even hesitate but hoisted Jo like a sack of feathers into the fork of a tree which she clung to, feeling her bruises. The whole thing added a bizarre touch, but now she saw it coming down through the trees and she sucked the air quickly into her lungs.

'Look out, Marsh, it's the staghound!'

He took a few steps forward, reaching for his hip knife.

The slobbering jaws were open and the tongue flicked the air around it. It stood above them watching intently, the dingo bitch commencing her descent.

'Don't move!' he ordered under his breath. 'Don't do anything until I tell you.'

'Can't you reach the rifle? Maybe I can!'

'*Don't move!*' he repeated, and the words blazed.

Jo sat bolt upright, her arms going limp around the tree. The dog was a killer of calves and small animals, but surely it wouldn't attack humans? Yet it was motionless, and the dingo kept edging in relentlessly. A trickle of sweat ran down between her eyes and she loathed having to sit there with Marsh on the ground, defenceless except for that knife.

'You need help!' she said crisply.

'Don't be so blasted silly!'

'Thanks!'

She kept still, her legs drawn up, the perspiration breaking out on her body. Both dogs looked ugly, cunning and powerful, eyes avid and predatory, creatures out of another world. A long moment passed and she couldn't stand it. At least she could hurl some stones at the dingo, the lesser evil. The kangaroo dog looked absolutely vicious, powerful enough to hunt and tackle the big reds and the rock wallabies and rip anything that attacked it in half. Abruptly she let go of the branch and plunged to the ground, and at the very same moment the staghound hurled its great body right at her, succumbing to the dreadful instinct for blood.

Fear seared right through her, then pain. Marsh literally threw her away, so she went sprawling right out on the sand, turning his body like a shield, tensing to take the full impact of the dog's massive body. It hit him and they rolled right down to the water's edge, the dingo bitch howling and coming dangerously close in defence of its mate, the muzzle drawn back in the familiar vicious threat.

Jo acted instinctively, slowed down by having the breath almost knocked out of her, but she managed to wave her arms violently in an attempt to check the animal to caution. It hesitated and she sprang to her feet, picking up a heavy slice of bark and hurling it. The brute changed direction.

'Savage. You savage!' she yelled, and it made away across the sand. '*Marsh!*'

He was lying on his back covered in blood, frightened and bruised. She rushed down to him and fell on her knees, eyes averted from the staghound's fallen body.

'You bloody little fool!' he said clearly.

Her eyes filled with tears and she bent down and kissed his mouth warmly, her eyes glistening, leaf green and highly charged with emotion. 'I think you're so brave!' she whispered.

'I suspect you're the same!'

'Is it dead?'

'Don't look so mournful!' he said dryly. 'It's kill or be killed. I wouldn't have liked to see you with a ravaged face!'

'But you're bleeding!' she agonised, her voice muffled and distraught.

'I'd die for you, baby!'

'Would you, Marsh?'

He groaned and sat up. 'This isn't *my* blood, green eyes. I'm still alive, strong and healthy. It's wonderful to have you looking at me like that, but I can't allow you to suffer such wretchedness!' He stood up and stripped off his shirt, hurling it backwards into the swamp. Jo's heart was beating furiously and she sat back on her ankles staring up at him. The silken bronze skin was without blemish, superbly taut, and she closed her eyes, quickening with a raw passion. It was a wonder he didn't notice it, because it was so strange. She couldn't seem to get up and she was trembling, deeply startled by her own feelings.

He looked down at her for a moment, black eyes searching, then finally he said: 'It's all right, Jo. Everything's all right. Come on, we'll go home!'

'Yes!'

The orchids he had gone to such trouble to collect for her were crushed to pulp. She still couldn't move, shaky with reaction, and he bent down and drew her to her feet, putting his arm around her shoulders and leading her back up the slope. Just a shoulder to lean on, that was all, but now she felt comfort, a deep sense of security that had her almost clutching him like he was something precious. From passion to comfort, both beautiful, the one ringed with fire, the other a quiet pulsing. He didn't seem at all strange to her, and he never would again.

CHAPTER SIX

THE morning began as it meant to go on—disastrously. Mrs McConnell's party was due in at eleven and Philippa in her capacity as close family friend piloted herself across from Summerfield with a whole cabin load of flowers she proceeded to arrange energetically a scant fifteen minutes after she arrived at the homestead. Obviously she was largely taken with her own capabilities and even began quizzing Ellen on the menus for lunch and dinner, suggesting changes. This was extremely ticklish, as anyone could have told her, but Philippa was totally unmoved by considerations other than her own.

Jo had made several attempts to keep out of her way, but finally she had to go downstairs. There she found the normally unflappable Ellen staring sightlessly at a painting, flushed and upset and a good ten years older. When she caught sight of Jo she wheeled around in relief, got a good grip on Jo's arm and pulled her into the walk-in pantry, where she shut the door and hissed her grievances.

'What's she *doing* here?'

Jo didn't quite pat her, but she looked as if she wanted to. 'Arranging the flowers. I have to say they look delightful.'

'Yes, all nice and neat around the edges. I like *your* arrangements, and I nearly opened my big mouth and said so. I just wish she'd keep out of my kitchen. I've been trying hard to keep my temper, but I tell you it's hard. Chicken doesn't suit her for lunch.'

'Really?' said Jo. 'She's too demanding for comfort.'

'Ah well,' Ellen moved a few jars and spoilt the whole effect, 'I'm not taking any notice. Mrs McConnell never had any complaints. I'm glad you're down, Jo. You'll be fully occupied coping with her. *I* can't!'

'Don't let her worry you, Ellen.'

'I *have* to!' Ellen's flush was betraying her blood pressure. 'She might be the next Mrs McConnell.'

Jo was shocked by the fiery lick of resentment she felt towards Philippa's aspirations. 'Do you think she has a chance?' she asked.

'She's got some hold on him!' Ellen said darkly. 'Otherwise, why should she be over here doing the flowers?'

'Why indeed!' Jo echoed, feeling nervy and un-resolved herself.

'Sweet as bush honey with Marsh!' Ellen went on, her face wrinkled with worry. 'You've seen her. She only shows her other side to the ones she doesn't think count. I can't pretend she doesn't upset me, but at least she could have the decency to allow me to get on with my work.'

'Can I help?' Jo offered.

'Thanks, Jo, but I'll manage. I always have done.' Ellen reached out humorously and patted Jo's arm. 'Just keep Miss Philippa Morley out of my way.'

'That might be a problem!' Jo said sincerely. 'I think she considers herself engaged to be married.'

'Well, I damned well won't dance at the wedding!' Ellen said resolutely, then suddenly laughed. 'There, now I feel much better!'

No sooner were the words out of her mouth like a blunder than there was the sound of breaking glass, a sad little wail abruptly cut off, then Philippa's voice giving vent to her feelings. She seemed to be an old hand at it, sufficient to send Jo and Ellen hurrying into the dining room to stem the tide of abuse. There they found Nara standing in an attitude of utter disgrace, beaten down by the tirade of sharp, hounding words, too spent with guilt to attempt an excuse. At her feet were the

scattered remnants of what had once been a green Mary
Gregory vase and a half dozen or more showy white
lilies with blooms at least nine inches across.

Philippa looked up as though she thought they had
arrived to support her. 'Just look what she's done!' she
snapped, tapping her long glossy fingernails on the polished credenza.

Ellen brooded on the spectacle, her flush mounting
alarmingly, and Jo, ever managing, decided to intervene.
'Go get a pan and brush, Nara. All we can do is clean it
up.'

Philippa made a sharp gesture to recall the young
lubra. 'You do realise the vase was quite valuable?'

'Right down to the dollar!' Jo answered wryly, something of an authority. 'These things happen.'

That wasn't good enough for Philippa, her triangular
face was a mask of hostility. 'She had no business touching anything. They never understand anything. They're
children in their simplicity. They simply don't know how
to take care of things.'

'I was only looking at the flowers!' Nara offered,
frightened and stammering. 'You came up behind me
and frightened me so. Them lilies are poisonous!'

'Are they?' Ellen's eyebrows shot up and it was apparent she accepted it.

'Yessum. I'm sorry!'

Philippa gave a contemptuous little laugh. 'Well,
really, we're not going to *eat* them!'

Jo took a few steps forward and put her hand on
Nara's arm. 'Do as I tell you, Nara. We'll have to clean
up here before Mrs McConnell arrives!'

'I can't see how you let her flounder around the house
at all!' Philippa continued compulsively, obviously not
through. 'There are so many things of value!'

Ellen's skin was beginning to look as if she had fallen
into a furnace. 'Look here, Miss Morley,' she said,

tightly exercising control, 'you seem to have a set on young Nara!'

Jo opened the door and pushed Nara out as she didn't seem able to go. 'It was very bad of me!' the young lubra wailed.

Jo shook her head and turned back to see Philippa staring at Ellen with cold eyes. 'That's simply not true, Ellen!' she said with quiet reason. 'I'm merely pointing out a few facts. The girl is careless. Look what she's done here. It's important to make a fuss before more things are broken. I'm just deciding whether to tell Mrs McConnell or not the minute she arrives.'

Ellen stood helpless for a moment, then her own position made itself manifest. 'Haven't you forgotten *I'm* the housekeeper here?'

'On the contrary,' said Philippa smoothly, not in the least disturbed, 'I know your position exactly, and there's always the possibility that it might change!'

Ellen's pleasant, lined face looked oddly stricken and Jo came to stand protectively beside her. 'Ellen, you're very busy. Why don't you let me clean up here?'

'Yes.' Ellen drew a deep breath, trying to calm herself. Philippa Morley, though she had invited herself, was still to be treated as a guest in the house. She got hold of herself and walked to the door just as Nara was returning. She took the dustpan out of her hand, passed it to Jo and dismissed the lubra with a nod of encouragement. Nara's narrow shoulders were heaving with repressed sobs.

The door closed and Philippa gazed down at the broken glass with absolute disapproval, kicking a piece towards Jo. 'Sometimes I wish Ellen would hurry up and retire. They get so troublesome at her age—ready to take offence at the least little thing!'

Jo moved forward on her knees, busy sweeping up jagged pieces. 'But she copes beautifully. Surely you wouldn't deprive her of a job?'

'We-ll,' Philippa considered. 'Someone younger and more used to handling staff would do better.'

Jo gripped the edge of the table for support. 'Are you serious?' She felt suddenly outraged, and she had a quick temper. 'You speak as though Ellen was a robot about to wear out. She gives her very best. She's a superb cook and all the house staff behave very nicely, yet you talk of dismissing her. I can't decide whether you're a busy-body or a heartless little snob. And while I'm at it kindly remember Nara is a human being, not a puppet that has to go *your* way. It's important to treat her people with dignity!'

Philippa spun around, looking absolutely affronted. 'Who the hell do you think you're talking to?' she demanded. 'How dare you talk to me like that? I've never heard such arrogance—and from an *employee*! I don't know how you were ever admitted to this house at all!'

'For a good reason—to take care of the children!'

Philippa's small face was burning with fury and a fever of jealousy. 'Don't think I accept that! I've learned a lot about you since you arrived.'

'What else is new?' shrugged Jo.

'Quite the comedienne, aren't you? Well, let me tell you . . .' She went to say more, but the sound of footsteps on the marble floor stopped her. Marsh had come down the stairway, heard the voices and walked through to the doorway, his eyes leaping over their faces and the reflection of tension in their bodies. 'What in the world is going on?' he asked mildly.

'Oh, Marsh!' Philippa clutched the credenza for a moment, then flew to him like a piteous kitten, her rosebud mouth quivering.

He slipped an arm around her automatically and held her. 'What *is* it?'

She gave a little choked sob, murmured something incoherent, and Marsh looked across at Jo. 'What's upset her?'

'Ah!' said Jo.

'A vase was broken!' Philippa answered, unutterably saddened.

'Is that all?'

'It was a valuable vase, Marsh. One of the Mary Gregorys.'

Marsh stared down at Philippa's auburn curls in blank amazement. He looked very tall and lean with Philippa clinging to his hard body, very dashing in a blue body shirt and beautifully tailored slacks in honour of his mother's arrival. 'My God, Phil, we can afford another!'

Philippa brought her head up appealingly and even Jo had to admit she did it supremely well. 'It wasn't only that, Marsh. Jo here seems to have taken a violent dislike to me. She called me a busy-body when I'm only trying to help!'

Jo swallowed at his expression and shook her head slightly. 'Not enough people have the courage of their convictions!' she declared bravely.

'And *you* do?' he asked dryly.

'You can't scare me, Marsh!' she said, 'and I'm not going to leave!'

'You could plan an apology!' Philippa suggested.

'You'll be waiting a long time. Now if you'll excuse me I'll just get rid of the broken glass. I won't be coming down to the airstrip. The children and I will stay here.'

'Suit yourself!' Marsh said shortly, his black eyes flashing so that he didn't look unlike Omar Sharif.

Philippa came out of her frightened child pose to look up brightly. 'I believe I've only Julie's bedroom to finish, then I'll join you, Marsh.'

'It was very thoughtful of you to go to so much trouble!' He found it necessary to make up for Jo's shortcomings and Philippa sparkled up at him, very chic this morning in a brief sundress with a bold jungle print and minus the matching jacket. She shot a triumphant look at Jo and danced out of the room.

Marsh bent down and picked up a stray sliver of glass. 'You pick a fine time to insult a family friend!'

'You bet!' retorted Jo. 'Listen, I'm not going to permit you to chat me up. Put me on bread and water if you like.'

'I think you deserve it.'

'I didn't expect you to listen to my side. Anyway ...' She broke off as Jenny surged into the room, not her usual charming and courteous little self.

'Paddy here?' she demanded abruptly.

'No,' said Jo.

'That's odd!'

'When did you last see him?' Jo asked.

'A long while ago. He could easily have sneaked out of the house. I've been trying to comfort Nara. She's crying.'

'Forget about Nara for a moment!' said Jo, instantly caught up by panic. 'What about Paddy?'

'I think he was going to pick you some flowers. Philippa didn't bother about your room and he thought it sort of shabby!'

'I'd better find him.'

Without another word to anybody Jo suddenly flew out the french door on to the veranda calling: 'Paddy ... Paddy!' waiting for the answer that never came.

Marsh was hard at her shoulder and she looked around quickly, her green eyes huge and anxious. 'You don't think he'd go down to the lake?'

Marsh took the stairs at a leap, clapping his hands so at least five boys working close to the house came to attention. 'Young Paddy!' he shouted. 'Find him. He's gone walkabout!'

Jo's vivid face was transformed. She found herself unable to speak. Paddy was her responsibility. She should have been watching him instead of indulging in a few stupid heated words with the likes of Philippa Morley, a spoiled rotten little heiress. 'He knows I like the blue lotus...' her face worked. 'Surely you don't think—?'

'Let's see!' He took hold of her hand and together they ran down the velvet slope of the lawn, long-legged Jo flashing beside him with fear as a spur. The peacock sky was cloudless above them. Flowers glowed in the sun. Nothing bad could happen on a day like this. All she could see was the water. Water ... water ... water. She felt ill. There was no sign of Paddy, and now the beautiful ornamental lake looked sinister its surface covered with the most exquisite quilt of lilies, ivory, pink and the heavenly lotus blue. It wasn't deep, but all water was dangerous to children. Paddy knew perfectly well that the lake was off limits unless accompanied, and he was usually so obedient.

No one ran from the house to tell them Paddy had been found and she came to a halt shaking with nerves, all her bright colour gone. 'I'm so frightened. Where could he be?'

Marsh didn't answer. She was conveying her feelings perfectly. He walked away calling Paddy's name while Jo dropped her head in her hands, knowing she was panicking but unable to check it. How could she ever face Anne and Dave again if anything happened to Paddy? He was unable to keep out of trouble. Every day invited fresh misadventures. She turned around and stared back over the gardens. Two boys were coming down on them now, their thin brown legs hurrying. There was some movement in one of the low bushes and she ran back up the slope.

'Paddy, is that you?'

After a minute a plaintive, faintly distorted little voice returned: 'Is that you, Aunty Jo? A bee stung me.'

'Oh, Paddy!' Relief surged through her like a shot of adrenalin. She raced around the beds crying: 'Didn't you hear us calling you?'

She found him sitting on the ground almost hidden from sight, his dear, chubby face streaked with tears, tender little mouth puffy and swollen grotesquely where a bee had stung him. 'Oh, Paddy!' She dropped to her knees hugging him emotionally. 'You've had us so worried!'

'I was trying to pick you some flowers, and a bee was waiting!' he wailed.

'And they're lovely!' Jo looked about at the colourful array already wilting in the sun. They were picked at all lengths of the stalk and some had no stalks at all.

'I forgot to tell you where I was going. I know you told me and Jenny wouldn't come. Nara's crying!'

'I'll have to tell Uncle Marsh!' She went to stand up, but Marsh was right behind her, his voice suggesting his relief.

'It's all right, I'm here. Well, young Paddy, you gave us all a splendid old turn. I feel at least ninety years old. Suppose we get you up to the house? I've got just the right antihistamine cream for that sting. When you're a little older we'll start you on a survival course!'

'Pick up the flowers, Aunty Jo!' Paddy mumbled.

'Yes, I will. They're lovely.'

Jo was trembling violently and Marsh put his hand on her shoulder to calm her, then he bent down and put his arms round Paddy, hoisting him on to his shoulder. 'Aren't you supposed to tell Aunty Jo where you're going?'

'Usually I do,' said Paddy quite truthfully. 'Gee, it's great up here. How tall are you, Uncle Marsh?'

'Six two. Just under two hundred pounds.'

'Gosh!' said Paddy as though he always suspected Uncle Marsh was Superman in disguise.

'That will give you something to work for. No more running off for you, young feller!'

'No, sir!'

'Jo, you can stop worrying,' Marsh turned to her. 'It's all over.'

'I did panic!' she said wryly.

'I know what you mean. You'd better get married and have kids of your own.'

'Will you marry me?' she asked flippantly, miraculously restored to lightness.

'What, and sacrifice my life for one moment of infatuation? Besides, I thought your feelings were engaged?'

'I set myself up for that one, didn't I?'

'You did!' His black eyes mocked her. 'Tell me, how do you feel on this momentous morning?'

'Nervy,' she confessed.

'Try to remember I'm not as tolerant as I look.'

'I'll be good!' she promised. 'We'd better hurry—I have to clean Paddy up before they arrive and he wants some cream on that poor little mouth.'

Marsh looked up at Paddy clutching him with both hands under his chin, told him to hold on, then dipped into his shirt pocket to fish something out and drop it gently over Jo's head. Both Paddy and Jo looked down with interest at a string of beautifully cut beryls of various colours and the naturally occurring tektite found on the plains of central Australia. The stones Jo could see glowed rose and pink and citrine and green and two shades of blue, linked together by a heavy gold chain. It was beautiful and very unusual.

'Wear it!' he said lightly, judging the effect of the stones against her bare skin. 'It's guaranteed to protect you from anything!'

'Will it kill bees?' Paddy's blue eyes flickered.

'Mosquitoes too,' said Marsh, his eyes meeting Jo's. 'It's a very powerful charm!'

She fingered the glittering strand. 'I don't mind humouring you in the least. We've been through a lot together.'

'Yes, sir! Sometimes a man can live a lifetime in a few days!'

Paddy rocked and swayed and Marsh threw his arms up and kept them there. 'Gee, you look pretty, Aunt Jo!' Paddy mouthed with some difficulty, absolutely delighted for her and fascinated with the glittering stones' potential.

'Yes, I think I'll change my clothes!' she said, her eyes glowing. 'I look more feminine in a skirt, and I have just the right outfit in mind.'

'Great!' Marsh cast up his eyes. 'That's your speciality, knocking us dead!'

'All right, so I didn't thank you!'

'Later will do!' he said, looking straight ahead, and she had the shivery notion that he could indeed cast a few spells.

They didn't come together properly until dinner time. Julie got off the plane looking frail and sickly and quickly sought the refuge of her room. Mrs McConnell, blooming like few women in their fifties did, tried to make up for it by being especially charming, and she had bought delightful presents for everyone including Jo, but the only alive thing about Blair was his eyes. The Outback might be doing wonders for Jo, but Blair looked like a fish out of water, slighter, whiter than Jo remembered, and she had remarked the way he quickly withdrew himself from the children's enthusiastic greeting, his face lifted towards Jo as though searching her heart and her soul. Blair never had enjoyed children. She was stuck with the thought and a far worse one.

In only a few short weeks a terrible thing had happened. She no longer loved him. It alarmed her, for it seemed to call attention to some monstrous emotional instability on her part. What was love anyway that it should blow hot and cold on the wind? The sight of him still moved her, the memory of what they had once been to each other, but she had distinctly changed. It almost seemed more appropriate to be sick with jealousy than feel she didn't really know her own mind. All these long years she had accepted that she loved him. She had limited herself and kept herself fine and pure, and now she was perfectly capable of greeting him with the same sort of feeling one reserved for a brother. And the black sheep of the family at that. It didn't make sense, and if it didn't make sense to Jo, it certainly didn't make sense to Blair, who had missed her unbearably both in and out of the shop. He would stop at nothing to tell her.

For dinner Jo got into the best outfit she had brought with her, a green transparent caftan over a strapless figure-hugging jersey sheath. She had put it in for the only reason that Anne had told her Marsh did a lot of entertaining from time to time, and what better time than now? Scattered lightly over the wispy chiffon were pairs of flowers in almost the same colours as her gemstone charm necklace, with the flowers bigger and bolder round the ankle-length hem. She had wound her long hair around heated rollers to give it more curl and she wore long gold pendant earrings that were actually Victorian, though she looked a very modern siren indeed.

Paddy was already tucked up asleep by the time she was ready to go downstairs and Jenny had had a lovely time watching her and was going to read in Jo's room for perhaps half an hour longer. 'Well, how do I look?' Jo turned around, one hand on her hip and the other languidly extended like a mannequin.

'Terrific!' Jenny studied her from the tip of her raven head to her gold-sandalled feet. 'Do you plan to marry Uncle Marsh?'

'Why do you ask?' Jo stopped whirling to put the question. It came out almost tremulous.

Jenny whistled, bright-eyed and breezy. 'I'm only fooling!'

'To begin with,' Jo said soberly, 'he's been spoken for!'

Jenny smiled at her, a very knowing, confidential smile as though she had a secret. 'I know more about Uncle Marsh than you do. If he asks you why don't you accept him?'

'Jenny dear, you're not thinking straight!'

'You look beautiful in that dress!' Jenny persisted. 'A knock-out drop. What's wrong with Julie?'

'Perhaps she's excited.'

'I thought only babies like Paddy got sick with excitement.'

'There *are* different stages,' Jo assured her. 'Now listen, you're going to turn the light off in another half an hour?'

'Promise!'

'What is it, anyway?'

'Oh, an adventure story.' Jenny held up her book by its cover.

'*Secret of the Cellar?* It sounds more like a ghost story,' Jo commented.

'No, it's one of a series. Just kid stuff. You can't take them seriously.'

Jo bent down to kiss the silky temple, clean and fresh-smelling from the bath. 'God bless. Call me if you need me.'

'It's all right!' Jenny looked up and smiled. 'Daddy always says the only time Paddy's safe is when he's tucked up in bed.'

'I hope his poor lip is down by the morning.'

Jenny was studying Jo's sumptuous swing of hair. 'He's had plenty of bee stings!' she said offhandedly. 'Do you think my hair needs cutting like yours?'

'Oh, I wouldn't!' Jo murmured persuasively. 'Plaits are always very nice for school. One has to keep tidy.'

'Yes, I suppose so!' Jenny agreed sensibly, 'though

nothing would surprise Miss Hathaway. She's seen every-thing!'

'I've a strange feeling I've been here before myself!' Jo walked to the door like a professional model, then turned around and smiled. 'Be good!'

'I *have* to!' said Jenny.

Evening found Julie a little improved, though she still looked far from well. Jo was as solicitous as everyone else and this seemed to surprise Julie, who kept casting her suspicious little glances from under her lashes. What-ever she was thinking it wasn't Beautiful Thoughts. Her summery flowered chiffon dress with ruffles was blue like her eyes and though it was very pretty and romantic she somehow looked washed out, without her usual sheen of health. To Jo's womanly eye she had undergone some indefinable change; more the neglected little wife than the radiant bride-to-be. It was obvious too that she was feeling extremely emotional, for her eyes glazed over from time to time as though it were possible she might burst into tears. The whole picture took Jo by surprise. She hadn't been expecting it.

Blair, however, had picked up considerably since his arrival. He looked his old self, smooth and elegant, beautifully tailored, attentive, well mannered, the perfect guest. Philippa, like so many other women before her, found him attractive and with her keen nose for intrigue she sensed something unlawful between Jo and Julie's fiancé. Situations were the spice of life to her and it was even possible she could turn this to her own advantage. Instinct warned her to fear Jo.

Ellen hadn't considered changing the menu. It was a tried and true one, suitable for a country house dinner, consisting of a delicious crab Mornay as an appetiser, a superb beef casserole served with fluffy rice, garlic bread and tossed green salad and her own rum cream pie for which she never handed around the recipe. Cheeses followed, the whole served with dry whites and dry reds from the family vineyards in the famous Barossa Valley. When she least expected it, Jo found she was enjoying herself immensely. The surroundings were splendid; they were using the formal dining room; and the food was excellent. She helped herself to liberal portions of everything, blessing the fact that she could at this stage of her life eat anything without her figure suffering disastrous results, while Marsh, looking more striking than ever, poured the wine.

Mrs McConnell, too, was in excellent spirits, fresh from her recent trip to Britain and a compulsive spending spree in Paris. Jo was sure her gown, and it couldn't remotely have been designated a dress, bore a French label. Cybill McConnell was still a very beautiful woman, but the beauty of middle age, not seeking any lost youth. She was tall and generously built but of fine proportions. She wore her luxuriant hair drawn back into a heavy chignon, a style she had never changed because it suited her perfectly. Her features were full but chiselled like a Roman statue and her magnificent dark eyes and her deeply moulded mouth were exactly reproduced in her only son. She looked what she was; a woman of intelligence and humour and breeding, and her love for her son, so natural and demonstrative, was returned in full measure.

Watching them both together, the pleasure they took in each other's company, the complimentary way the one had of picking up where the other left off or pointing up the other's stories, Jo was reminded yet again of the things she had missed in her own life. She had only been a small girl when her mother had deserted her and her father had made no effort to foster either her love or her friendship. He simply had no need of her, and Aunt Elizabeth and Uncle Joss had been there to fill the gap. At least Aunt Elizabeth had forgiven her, for Blair had brought with him one of his mother's long rambling letters filled with all the news and asking Jo's advice in certain matters. She would have to reply.

Mrs McConnell, at the end of the table opposite her son, dominated the conversation. She was in fine form and she obviously felt the need to get to know Jo better, because she addressed her constantly, liking Jo's sense of humour which was naturally displayed by Jo's laughing appreciatively at all Mrs McConnell's sallies and accounts of recent experiences at home and abroad. Towards the end of the sweet course, the conversation turned to more serious matters and Marsh introduced the current uranium controversy with a brief reference to the mineral deposits they had already assured him existed on Malakai.

Blair retreated. He was not in the least politically minded or a serious, responsible individual, for that matter. Philippa was uninterested, being exclusively self-orientated, and Julie, who had been remarkably silent right through the meal, suddenly pushed back her chair and asked:

'Would you all excuse me? I'd like to take a walk.'

Mrs McConnell busy summoning her arguments looked up in astonishment. 'Right now, dear?'

'Just a little air. I've been feeling off colour all day.'

Both men were standing now, Marsh staring at his cousin rather fixedly, Blair seemingly embarrassed.

'Why, of course, dear! How thoughtless of me!'

'Please, Aunty Cybill—all of you!' Julie appealed to them. 'Finish your dinner!'

Blair actually looked as if he intended doing just that, and Marsh put his arm around Julie, his black eyes ranging round the flower and candle-decked table. 'Leave this to me!'

He looked so splendidly competent that Blair sat down again and his mother called after him, 'Darling, what about coffee on the veranda? Julie, would you like that, dear? I'll have it brought out.'

'That would be lovely, Aunty!' Julie said mournfully, her fragile frame almost hidden from view by Marsh's broad shoulders and back.

They went out and Mrs McConnell frowned down at her empty plate. 'Poor little thing. Perhaps it's nerves!'

Blair tried to look suitably worried and Jo could have kicked him. 'She's been doing a lot of running around lately!' he explained. 'Shopping for her trousseau, that kind of thing. Perhaps I should go to her?'

Jo's green eyes sparkled the answer to that, but he carefully looked away from her for perhaps the first time that evening. She looked like a slender goddess, and she couldn't have worn a more flattering dress. The green transparent chiffon made great play of her beautiful figure, all fluid sinuosity, and something had awoken in her all her old vivacity. He knew damn well he was going to find out. Having had her love and allegiance for so long, he couldn't permit her to get away from him.

Philippa, on Jo's right, didn't know exactly what was going on, but she had a great sense of direction. Her topaz eyes glittered and she stared hard at Blair. Compared to Marsh he wasn't in the least handsome or distinctive and he had no physique to speak of. She stared harder. He *was* sexy, with those hooded eyes and that faintly crooked smile, and he was interested in ... Philippa had a pretty good idea ... Jo. If she was right, small wonder Julie hadn't been able to finish her dinner.

Mrs McConnell was still brooding over Julie's nerves and Jo addressed her directly. 'Shall I ask Ellen to serve coffee outside? She's probably loading the trolley to bring it in here.'

Cybill looked up and smiled, and Marsh's resemblance to his mother was unmistakable if only through the eyes and the mobility of the shapely mouth and certain shared gestures. 'Thank you, Jo, but I'll have a word with her. Dinner was superb and I'd like to tell her so. Ellen is a treasure. It makes me happy to know she's here looking after Marsh.' She went to rise and Blair moved swiftly to hold her chair. She gave him a less expansive smile than the one she had given Jo, moving out of the room at a regal glide, leaving the mature intoxication of Bulgarian rose and jasmine.

Philippa too began to excuse herself, her tiny smile suggesting that by staying she would be playing gooseberry. 'You don't mind?' she said archly.

Blair wasn't so sleepy-eyed that he couldn't see the malice behind the smile. He had even been wondering why she was staring so hard. 'We'll join you soon on the veranda.'

Philippa walked to the great cedar double doors that separated the formal dining room from the main drawing room, then turned to look back at them. 'No hurry. You must have lots to catch up on.'

'And why not?' Blair rejoined smoothly. 'Jo and I grew up together. We've worked together for years.'

'I didn't know!' said Philippa.

Jo almost burst out laughing at her expression. 'Is it a cause for such disappointment?' she asked.

'But it's not really that, is it?' Philippa couldn't resist a little thrust. It was surprising how effective a few stabs in the dark could be. She looked very pretty standing there against the polished doors flanked by bronze figures holding aloft candelabra. Her topaz eyes never left them, taking on the colour of the clinging geranium-coloured dress she wore. If there was going to be any scene it was unnatural for her to want to miss anything.

'Anything wrong?' Jo asked dryly.

'I'll let you know!' Philippa waggled her fingers and drifted away like a blossom.

'Is she usually so bitchy?' Blair asked, turning back to the table.

'She's got a great nose for scandal.'

'Well, she's not on her own there. How are you, Jo? I mean, how are you really?'

'You see me!' she said lightly. 'I feel fine.'

'You look divine,' he assured her.

'That's encouraging.' It was odd for her to start feeling bored, but she did.

'Be serious, Jo!' he said 'savagely. 'God, how I've missed you!'

'Your mother tells me you've already found my replacement.'

'What did you expect? I can't handle it all on my own. Olive quit, by the way. You always were her darling. I hope she goes ahead without a reference. Anyway, business is booming. I've had two important briefs in the last week—connections of Julie's.'

'More to the point, what's wrong with her?' asked Jo.

'How should I know!' He picked up his wine glass and put it down again. 'One can't ignore wealth, can one? It gives an aura. The furnishings in this room alone would cost a small fortune. The whole place is right up my street, but not in this godforsaken location. It'll be years before I come back again. As for Julie—well, I suppose she's got problems.' There was a decided hint of sourness about this and Jo said quietly:

'What made you like this? If you can't use your heart try using your head. She *is* your fiancée. Presumably she's going to give you the chance to use her money, trusting girl. If I were you I'd make a fuss of her. She looks slightly neglected.'

There was a fine tremor in Blair's slender hand. 'She's not quite as I thought!' He glanced at her, silently appealing for support. 'In her own way she's even ruthless!'

Jo sat up then, looking unconvinced.

'It would serve you right if she was! But I don't believe it. A little bit of a thing like that!'

'She knows what she wants, and what's more she knows how to get it!' Blair persisted in a leaden tone.

'And how is she making sure of you? By setting up

commissions, ensuring all your dreams of success come true. You *are* having a hard time of it. In return the very least you can do is follow her out when she feels ill!'

He held up a protesting hand. 'Don't, Jo. The last weeks have been deadly.'

'I'm sorry, I really am. I'm not your enemy, Blair,' Jo assured him, 'not now or ever. I'll always remember the good times, the way you were all so kind to me.'

It was obvious he was taken aback, even glaring at her. 'How are you making it with McConnell?' he demanded.

'I beg your pardon!' She was insulted more on Marsh's behalf than her own.

'You're too much, Jo, do you know that? A very funny girl. You're twenty-five and you still haven't fulfilled yourself as a woman.'

'You mean I never did sleep with you?' she said, going right to the point.

'Maybe I didn't press it enough!' His hooded eyes gleamed with triumph. 'Don't tell me McConnell knows how to behave himself?'

'He does. I don't!' Jo said with a tantalising smile. 'You've only to give me the chance!'

Blair shoved his glass away. 'What are you saying?'

Deliberately she veiled her green eyes. 'Nothing that should properly interest you. Shall we rejoin your fiancée?'

She stood up and he came round and closed in on her. 'Jo, I have to talk to you.'

'I must regretfully decline with my best manners. What's wrong with both of you, anyway? Haven't you come out here to plan a wedding?'

'I don't know!'

He was staring at her, the muscles of his jawline working, and she wondered how she had ever got over him, but she had. 'You aren't your usual self, are you?' she said kindly.

'Have you missed me at all?'

She started to move back a discreet distance. 'I don't even know where the days have gone. I've been fully occupied.'

'I don't mind waiting!' he said in a low, tense tone. 'You still love me, Jo. You never change.'

'Everyone changes!' she said decisively, because she had found it was true.

'I realise what I've lost!' Blair's little-boy expression was giving him an added attraction, but Jo was unmoved.

'Keep it up and you'll have me crying!'

His flickering eyes betrayed a rising temper. 'That necklace, where did you get it?' He moved to stand in front of her.

Jo shrugged without bothering to answer and he caught her high up on the arm. 'I've never seen it before and I know every single thing you own.'

'You missed this,' she said dryly.

'I see!' His eyes narrowed to dangerous slits. 'Don't *do* this to me, Jo!'

'Oh, shut up!' She leaned backwards, and behind them somebody laughed, a conspiratorial giggle.

Blair dropped his hand and turned around, his expression ugly. 'Do you do this for nothing or do you get paid?' he demanded.

Philippa, with a real chance at mischief, merely smiled like a cat after cream. 'Coffee is served. I just came to tell you.'

'Thank you!' Blair took Jo's hand and pressed it to his side. 'We're just coming.' He was already sick to death of Philippa and her bright knowing glances. In fact he could have struck her with a tightly clenched fist. Bitchy, malicious women were the last straw, and somehow Jo had made an enemy of her. This line of thought could only lead him one way—sexual competitiveness and a fancied invasion of territorial rights. Miss Philippa

Morley had her flag firmly planted on Malakai and McConnell. How he envied him a whole batch of attributes, his vitality and his money—but he wasn't going to have Jo. Blair had always found it hard to let anything get away from him, and now it seemed he was running the grave risk of losing Jo. He didn't see anything extraordinary in his own behaviour. Plenty of men he knew had their cake and ate it too. With Jo back in the company he could have everything he had built and worked for. Jo was a fascinating woman and his finely tuned instinct told him she was attracted to McConnell whether she knew it or not. He had to take measures, but it would probably be tomorrow. He couldn't risk a confrontation in the house. One false move could ruin him and McConnell was watching him like a hawk.

Jo recalled that the rest of the evening passed as though they were all wearing masks. A decided constraint had come into the atmosphere, and Philippa's odd little remarks multiplied the effect, always with Jo as their focus. She seemed not to care that she was coming dangerously close to further upsetting Julie, who was looking paler than ever, and eventually Mrs McConnell decided they should all retire early—it was wonderful how refreshing a good night's sleep could be, and similar expressions out of the countless varieties. Blair knew he ought to be careful, so he followed the others upstairs, but Marsh caught hold of Jo's arm, staying her progress.

'I want to get a few things cleared up!' he announced.

She actually shuddered because there was a sardonic aloofness in his expression. 'You're the boss!' she shrugged.

'You use that word easily.'

'Isn't it the truth?'

Philippa, it seemed, was listening again. She came back into the room for a last good night, heartened by the friction in the atmosphere. Nothing suited her better

than clashes, and Marsh and Jo seemed on the verge of a
fierce quarrel. If so, her strategy had worked. All she
needed to do now was drop a necessary word in Mrs
McConnell's ear. Cybill was very fond of her niece and if
she knew Julie's fiancé had leanings towards his former
associate, it was unlikely that Jo Adams would remain
around long.

Philippa stood upon tiptoe and touched her mouth to
Marsh's tantalising smooth, dark jawline. It was a compulsive thing. She was mad about him and always had
been, and she began to tremble with the force of the
emotion that gripped her.

'Any plans for the morning, darling?'

'Bart has about twenty or thirty brumbies lined up to
bring in. There's some talk of going out in the morning. I
haven't decided yet.'

'If you do, may I come?'

'Certainly.'

Philippa took a few steps backwards and her whole
expression changed. 'Good night, Jo.'

A considerable barrier was between them and Jo
didn't smile, neither did she sound cold and allow Philippa to emerge victorious. 'Pleasant dreams!'

Philippa withdrew because she had to, and Jo shut her
eyes briefly. Marsh had taken on his piratical *persóna*,
tougher, infinitely more formidable, and no damned nonsense. He let her remain like that for a few moments,
then he swung her around.

'Did you have to wear that damned dress?' he demanded.

She was startled and looked it. 'And what's the nature
of your complaint?'

'I was hoping you could see it without having to point
it out!'

'Well, I can't!' she said stiffly. 'What's wrong with
it?'

For an answer he swung her round to face a long gilded

wall mirror decorated in the same manner as the French Empire chairs. 'I don't see anything wrong?'

'You're not looking properly. It's an extremely distracting dress.'

'Your mother said she loved it!'

'Certainly. My mother is an angel!'

For all his curt manner and the brilliant glitter of his eyes Jo had the weirdest sensation of being embraced. 'Hang on a second!' she said tightly because she thought she was melting. 'You thought I wore it as a calculated gesture?'

'Didn't you?'

'It was the best dress I could afford, and it goes with my magic charm.'

He shrugged and his shapely mouth thinned. 'To be quite frank I'm not sure which way it's working. Come on,' he urged her. 'I want to get out of here.'

'First tell me what you're up to?'

'I don't have to. In the field of getting my own way I'm an expert, so for God's sake don't struggle.'

Jo allowed herself to be hustled out of the house, down the front steps and into the Range Rover standing in the drive. 'With respect, Mr McConnell, would you consider telling me where we're going?'

'Does it matter? Anywhere we go we're on Malakai. There are a few things I want you to understand and I didn't want to talk at the house.'

'Obviously whatever it is you're uptight!'

'I'll tell you this, I've never seen such a mess!' he snapped.

He was handling the vehicle expertly, flicking his way through the gears with absent practised skill. Jo stole a look at his profile. It wasn't conventionally handsome like Blair's, but splendidly rugged. She felt extraordinarily restive and she had to admit dreadfully excited, a disturbing anticipatory thing as if he might make love to her again when from his violent, brooding expression he was considering no such thing. She slid further down in the seat, waiting for him to tell her.

It was the most beautiful night, with a breeze blowing in the scent of boronia, a night of magic with small pulsing camp fires through the trees, the sound of voices and a shivery female chant to keep harm away from the camp. They were moving along at about forty miles an hour and Marsh was maintaining this speed, the expression on his dark face fixed and tense, a vertical frown between his black brows. Every point, every sandhill, slope and flat was illuminated by the moon, the curving river and the tributary creeks shining silver, the flower-sprinkled gums etched in darkly, their bases lost in shadows. It was all so vast, so empty, they might have been lost on the moon, and with intense shock Jo at last realised that whatever she had felt for Blair was as nothing compared to the fervour she felt for this man. She didn't understand it, and she still felt defiant about it, even reckless. The night was inducing a taunting intimacy and she wasn't the untouchable creature she once was. Marsh had already shown her her own sensuality and she was poised on a knife edge, wanting and not wanting ... yearning yet insecure. She knew very little about what he really thought.

When he finally pulled up she turned to him in surprise. She didn't recognise the territory at all. They were well beyond the camp fires and out on the mulga plains, where a rain storm had covered the countryside in a beautiful yellow bottlebrush with a delicate, delicious scent.

'Well?' she asked, almost whispering because everything was so quiet.

He frowned and shook his head almost as if he wished to spare her. 'Julie's pregnant!'

'God!' she gasped.

'That's what I said.'

She turned her head swiftly and looked out the window. 'When did she tell you?'

'She never said a word. I asked her.'

'Poor Julie!' she sighed.

He made no reply for a moment, then he insisted she turn around. 'That's really very compassionate of you, Jo. It's one way of making sure of a man.'

She glanced at him and away again. 'What do you want me to say?'

'Oddly, nothing. Just accept it.'

'Does Blair know?'

'I doubt it, but I'd like to be around when he's told. I've an idea he might blame Julie entirely.'

'Maybe it's a good thing!' she said heavily.

'Knowing Julie, she probably gave it a bit of thought. She's a mixture, is Julie. She loves him and she wants him. All her life she was managed very strictly, and now she's jumped in for herself. I can't say I approve or even see the wisdom of her actions. I think she has the notion that this will solve everything. To be frank, she feared you, so she didn't hesitate to commit herself and Leighton. It's an ancient trick.'

'Does your mother know?' Jo asked in a low voice.

'I've asked Julie to be good enough to tell her. Mother had everything planned, you know—a big wedding.'

'Well, it can still go through,' she said almost harshly, scarcely looking at him.

'Have a good cry!' he invited.

'I'll do nothing to please you!' she burst out in agitation, opening the door and jumping out and giving the door a good hard slam after her. Why did she expect any sort of sympathy or understanding from Marsh? Blair would probably go round the bend when he heard, and she experienced a quick rush of malicious pleasure because he deserved a good fright. No wonder Julie had looked sickly and triumphant at once, and probably she would make a good little mother. Her way, however, Jo considered the ultimate in madness. It seemed so much better to wait and plan for a longed-for child. Blair, the rake, she thought, utterly disenchanted. Could there be anything more normal than a wife and a mistress, both doing their best to hold his interest? Tears stung her eyes at the whole sorry mess, even when now she found herself utterly neutral.

Curiously the tears slid down on her cheeks and she walked away quickly thinking of Aunt Elizabeth and Uncle Joss and how Aunt Elizabeth's jaw would fall, even though she was in favour of being a grandmother. She was walking quite blindly, the breeze blowing her hair and her caftan away from her body. Love was a jungle, but obviously Julie meant to survive it. With her love for Blair a dead thing, Jo sincerely hoped she would. She didn't envy Julie her task of telling the great news to her aunt. Having a baby was no ordinary nervous crisis. She even wondered fleetingly if Julie had proved agreeable to Blair in bed. Ah well, it was their problem now . . .

Still the tears came, falling like jewels. Maybe they were tears of self-pity for the waste of precious time. The crushed wildflowers under her feet were as sweet as freesias. She needed Marsh desperately, but he wasn't going to disturb her. Actually he was Philippa's man and she was a two-time loser.

She almost fell over the new-born colt curled in a depression and cushioned by brush. Even by day he would have been well camouflaged. Her heart lifted with shock, but the little creature didn't attempt to wobble to its feet. It just raised its head. 'Oh, you adorable little thing!' She fell to her knees and called back to Marsh, so entranced with her find that her mood changed miraculously and the sparkling fount of tears dried up.

He'd been watching her, giving her time, then suddenly he was behind her, lifting her away instantly and keeping his arms around her. 'For God's sake, Jo, you don't want to tangle with an irate mother!'

'Then where is she?' she asked.

'Not too far distant. Don't worry about that. All wild

mares go off alone to give birth. As soon as the foal can manage its legs she takes it back to the herd. Let's get out of here.'

Jo held on to his hand, lifting her head to look back at him. 'Just a little longer. Look, it's trying to get to its feet. How old do you suppose it is?'

'A day or two.'

'I'm going to come back with my camera.'

'That's what you think!' He bore her backwards and suddenly without warning a wild mare came rocketing out of a distant clump of trees, charging them in defence of her foal, silvery grey in the moonlight with a dark mane and tail.

'Run!' he said in a voice that didn't brook argument.

She had a wild impulse to drag him with her, but he wasn't coming. The mare was pounding towards them with dynamic energy, a unique creature, unbroken and free, beautiful and dangerous in its flight. The little colt had wobbled to its feet and was standing quietly, but the mother ignored it for the moment, pondering the human presence and what she was going to do about it.

With her heart racing, Jo reached the safety of the vehicle, and fell against it, turning back to look for Marsh. Any horse was highly strung and a wild horse extremely apprehensive. It was a moment for facing facts and she was desperately anxious for Marsh, who was moving back slowly towards her. Somehow he had stopped the mare's headlong charge, but it was facing him boldly, only a short distance dividing them. In staying, in wanting a few minutes longer, she had put him at risk. Her heart went out to him, beating violently. If he suffered any harm she couldn't endure it. Only the realisation that any movement on her part would act as a spur to the mare kept her hugging the door of the jeep.

The mare seemed to remain in a trancelike state while Marsh kept moving slowly backwards, not showing the slightest sign of turning and running as she had done. By the time he reached her she was exhausted by her panic. It didn't seem possible that such raw and violent aggression could be soothed by talking an animal around. She had seen Ned's demonstrations, but this was something else again.

'All right?' He touched her shoulder and as in all moments of crisis Jo reacted flippantly.

'Never a dull moment around here!'

'It's not the concrete jungle, you know!'

'No, it's wonderful!' She experienced a deep sense of easement.

He shook his head slowly. 'You've been crying,' he accused.

'So I'm disfigured!'

'No, you're dazzling, and you're going to create quite a situation if you're not careful.'

'*I'm* not the one who likes dabbling in intrigue!' she said shortly. 'What about your girl-friend?'

'She's just a little spoilt!' he said as though he couldn't care less.

Under the impetus of its mother's butting head the colt wobbled to its feet again and followed the mare's lead towards the clump of trees and nearer the home range. It seemed an especially poignant scene and both of them broke off their verbal sparring to look at it. 'You could have been badly injured!' Jo said softly, and shivered.

'I've been in worse situations,' he shrugged. 'The vital thing, the *absolutely* vital thing, is not to panic because it can have disastrous repercussions. All animals can be made to respond to man if he understands them.'

'Well, it was a valuable lesson for me!'

'And there's another that can't afford to wait. You just have to abdicate.'

'So Julie's major gamble can come off. Who'd want to spoil it?' The vital thing was not to give herself away.

She could still keep pretending she hadn't outgrown her girlhood folly. He was wrong, completely wrong, only now she felt like running away.

She reached for the door handle and he turned her around as if it was inevitable she had to pay the price.

'What about that thank-you for your necklace?'

'But it didn't save me!'

His eyes travelled over her face—the luminous eyes, the straight nose, the firm chin, the full curved mouth. 'That's why I'm here—to do that.'

'And you're no amateur! Very well,' she murmured, 'thank you!'

'And you haven't one chance in a hundred million of getting away.'

The way he drew her into his arms was perfectly in character with the minimum of fuss and the maximum emotional apparatus of masculine power. It was brilliant, and Jo saw that it was a mistake to deny him. His mouth closed over her own and a hundred little fires began to glow inside her. She was hungry for this. It was unnerving, and she couldn't resist the dangerous impulse to respond absolutely.

He held her away from him and looked down at her curiously. 'You're a very clever girl, Josephine!'

'You may be right!' She knew she was acting like a siren, but she resolutely steered away from telling him she loved him. 'So what happens now?'

The flash in his eyes was quickly hidden. 'I haven't finished with you yet!' he said lightly, and slipped a hand around her nape, holding her head up. 'Sometimes a woman can seem like a miracle.

'Can't we just leave it?' she said pleadingly, when she had come burningly alive. 'I don't want complications.'

'Of course you do!' he said gently, and before she could stop him, he claimed her mouth again until she was lying against him, repeating his name over and over.

CHAPTER SEVEN

No chubby hand woke Jo in the morning, no ear ringing, no little voice admonishing her to get up before the sun burned a hole in her. When Jo looked in on the children they were both sleeping peacefully like cherubs. The first excitement of being on the station was gradually wearing off and they were settling to a more relaxed routine. They had appealed to Uncle Marsh to have at least one night sleeping out under the stars, but the time wasn't right with guests in the house. Perhaps next week; Jo was looking forward to it herself.

She dressed quickly in a soft embroidered voile peasant blouse and a brilliantly patterned skirt, then went out into the hallway, her head a little heavy because she had slept badly, the odd dream peopled by Blair and Julie having a very convincing argument, over *her*. It didn't make for a quiet night. Further down the corridor Mrs McConnell emerged from her room, saw Jo and signified by way of a hand signal that she wished her to come to her room.

My first greeting of the morning, Jo thought, and it has to be silent. She followed Mrs McConnell's gorgeous retreating figure into the master bedroom suite. So far she had only looked very briefly into it. It included a sitting room, separate dressing rooms and a large master bathroom. The ceilings were high, with heavy ornamental beams, the wall-to-wall carpet a soft seductive pale gold to match the drapes and the silk brocade bedspread, and the furnishings and paintings, the white marble fireplace, were all beautiful and distinctive. Jo would have enjoyed it a lot more, but it was obvious from Mrs McConnell's expression that she had some pressing worry on her mind.

She waved Jo into a Louis XV chair, a fine piece, but not the most comfortable in the world, considering what she must say, and Jo, being Jo, decided to help her.

'Is anything the matter?' she asked kindly.

Mrs McConnell drew her magnificent Oriental kimono more closely around her. 'The fact is, Jo,' she said in her rich contralto, 'both Julie and Philippa have come to me with the most disquieting news!'

Jo's stomach sank, though she looked up and said dryly: 'I already know Julie's news. Marsh told me. But I think I'd dismiss anything Philippa might have to say.'

Mrs McConnell inclined her splendid dark head, dressed appropriately enough in a thick pigtail. 'Actually, I'm rather cross with Philippa. What she told me,' she glanced up quickly with Marsh's brilliant, penetrating gaze, 'is it true?'

'Perhaps you'd better tell me what she *did* say?'

'I'm past caring now!' Mrs McConnell said with bitter humour. 'First things first. There's Julie. Could you please tell me, Jo, if you ever loved Blair?'

'If it's just between you and me, Mrs McConnell. I don't trust anyone else!'

Mrs McConnell raised her head. 'I'd feel exactly as you do. But I'm not a gossip, thank God!'

'There was a time when I was in love with Blair,' Jo admitted.

'And did Blair give you to understand...' a Gallic gesture ... 'you know what I mean!'

'I'm paying you the compliment of being completely honest with you. Blair and I spoke of marriage. At that time I thought it was all I ever wanted. The engagement party, for instance, wasn't very nice for me, but looking back, and it's not so very long ago, it seems I was a different person. It's difficult to explain, but I'm no longer *in* love with him. I think I ought to continue to love him as family. And that's what the Leightons have been to me—family. One learns, and then Blair taught me a lot about the business!'

'Yes,' Mrs McConnell said crisply. 'It would give me great satisfaction to kick his behind, but he *is* brilliant. If it were only brilliance! I tell you, Jo, this morning I feel like an elderly woman. We have a position to keep up!'

'Even so, these things happen in all circles,' Jo pointed out.

Mrs McConnell let out a long whistling breath. 'I'd really rather it hadn't happened this way. Julie has given me to understand it was no accident, but planned. It was difficult to know what to say to her. It seems ridiculous now, but I always thought butter wouldn't melt in her mouth. The whole thing is a matter of how one has been brought up. I so dislike anything *seedy*. Poor little thing, she needs me now. You realise, of course, that Blair doesn't know?'

'Then he'll have to be told!' Jo returned rather acidly. 'I mean, he was there at the time.'

'I should say so—and he didn't act properly!' Mrs McConnell closed her eyes briefly and her head fell forward on her chest. 'I'm so glad the thought of their marriage doesn't make you unhappy, Jo. I like you. Goodness knows what Philippa hoped to gain. I might tell you she upset me. Bystanders should keep safely out of these things!' She paused and went to the long windows, looking out. 'It was going to be one of the biggest events on the social calendar. Now I'd like to wave them off today!'

'You should refuse to allow it to upset you,' Jo said gently. 'It will work, you'll see, and when the baby comes everyone will be happy.'

'The extraordinary thing is, I half expected it,' Mrs McConnell mused. 'Even before she got it out I half expected it. Strange little girl. She's always been very repressed. I suppose we all break out finally. I did expect better behaviour, but however—! I do hope she finds comfort in this marriage she's set on. She'll always have to keep an eye on him. Ingratitude, ingratitude, but still it's no tragedy. Nothing's considered a mistake these days. I was brought up to believe that a woman should come to her marriage with her honour intact. All the young ones just go ahead, and really they're just as ignorant of human relationships as ever their parents were. I don't give a damn about Blair,' she went on, 'but I was worried about you. Really, Philippa told me an intolerable lie. I'm so disappointed and irritated. I don't like deliberate mischief!'

Jo said, 'Perhaps she thought she was being helpful.'

'I don't think so. At least it didn't strike me that way. I'm so glad dear Grandfather isn't alive. Really, he would have been *seething*! Family celebrations were for everyone's benefit. Not a one of us would have dared embarrass him.' Mrs McConnell passed a weary hand over her eyes, then she looked down at Jo with a curious intimacy. 'I want to have another chat with you, but about more pleasant matters. If you're going downstairs, dear, could you please ask Ellen to send a tray up to my room. I'm not yet ready to face the world or even decide what we must do, but at least I know you're not part of some dreadful triangle. You're too good for Blair. I admire him in many ways, but I can't help saying it. Whether he's going to be good for Julie or not, she wants him, otherwise we wouldn't be in the predicament we're in. Motherhood may be good for her. It will give her something to do!'

Jo stood up and went to the door. 'I'll tell Ellen right away.'

Mrs McConnell put up a staying hand. 'It might be an idea if Julie had something brought up to her before she stirs!'

She was trying to be calm, but Jo could see she was very upset. She smiled understandingly, then gently closed the door. She had a certain sympathy for every-

body but not Blair. On the whole, Blair's behaviour had
been deplorable and she wanted to tell him so, but she
knew that if she did he would only look at her with that
faintly crooked smile. Blair made his own rules and just
as easily abandoned them, but it would be impossible for
him to get out of this situation. Jo was suddenly, furiously glad.

She gave Ellen Mrs McConnell's message, had a com-
panionable cup of coffee with her in the kitchen where
Nara and another little housegirl were busy helping out,
then she decided on a walk around the garden and down
to the ornamental lake, a favourite spot. Nara had already promised to keep her eye on the children, and in
any case they were yet to get up and have their breakfast. Julie's news had brought everything to a head. Both
Marsh and Mrs McConnell felt responsible for Julie and
were unhappy at the course she had decided on, but Jo
wasn't going to see it as her fault. She had a good idea of
the kind of thing Philippa would have said, though
apparently Philippa had received quite a different re-
ception from the one she expected.

Her head felt easier now and she threw up her face to
the morning, her hair lifting on the strengthening breeze.
This was a beautiful time of the day, radiant and cool,
before the sun swung into full power. She moved down
the green lawn and around the flower beds, bending
down and looking around appreciatively at the ecstasy
of flowering, waving to a small black boy who smiled
shyly, then twisted and ran away.

She had been down at the lake for almost an hour
before Blair joined her. He had seen her from the balcony of his room and his need to talk to her was urgent.
She seemed to be in a state of silent meditation and she
looked very beautiful and almost remote, the sunlight
shafting through the trees touching her golden-olive skin
and deepening her eyes to jade. She didn't even know he

was there until he threw a fallen blossom in her direction. Immediately her eyes became guarded and her dreamy half smile vanished.

'Hello there!' she said doggedly.

'*Jo!*'

It sounded very emotive and she stared at him hard. He was immaculately groomed as always, but there were interesting shadows beneath his eyes.

'Is anything wrong?' He flared up instantly at the quality of her expression, detecting the criticism.

'Wrong?' Her delicate brows rose.

'You're looking at me very strangely.'

'I hope you don't mind. You've been acting sort of strangely lately. In fact, even talking to you is a dangerous proposition,' she confessed.

His lean face flushed angrily. 'Half your trouble is, Jo, you're too damned old-fashioned. You make difficulties and you put your whole soul in to it. It goes oddly with your beautiful body!'

She looked down at the lotus blossoms standing up waxily in their violet blue haze. 'Look, Blair, I want to tell you something. You're determined on your marriage, aren't you?'

'Oh, yes!'

'No regrets?'

'You know damn well what they are!'

'I'm not flattered!' she shrugged.

'You know why? You plague yourself with scruples.'

'I do!' she said spiritedly. 'I admit it.'

'Anyway,' he said after a minute, 'I've already spent a good deal of money.'

'Surely you could have waited?'

'I didn't *want* to!' he said, irritated by her attitude. 'I'll treble Julie's share in the business in under a year!'

'Well, if it's not worrying her, why should it worry me?' Jo said briskly. 'Be good to her, Blair. If you are, she'll stick to you no matter what!'

'I know that!' he said in a throttled voice. 'It's *you* I want to talk about. Come back to the firm, Jo. You could quite easily. Julie won't bother us with tiresome jealousy. You have tremendous flair and all the clients and manufacturers like you. We all enjoy having you around.'

She paused and said jauntily, 'Well, I've been thinking a lot about it and I've decided to open my own business!'

He gave a bored smile and flicked an insect away from the open neck of his shirt. 'You know better than that. You're good, but you're not that good. Besides, you haven't got a cent!'

'Maybe like you I've found myself a backer,' she said coldly.

Flames shot into his amber eyes. 'Go on!' he invited. 'This beats me hollow!'

'If you're waiting for me to tell you, I'm not going to. That's my business!'

Blair's lips tightened and his well-bred face whitened. 'You haven't been misspending your time, have you?'

'No!' she said, watching him lose control. Blair, the ruthless, jealous egotist.

A wave of fury took possession of him. 'Is it possible McConnell's already your lover?'

'I intend him to be!' Jo said sweetly, pressing him to the limit.

She saw his face, but she couldn't move quickly enough. His sweeping slap stung viciously across her cheek and twisted her head back so that she didn't see her rescuer until he had pushed Blair in the lake. '*Paddy!*' Her voice trembled weakly and she was dismayed that he had witnessed the scene.

'It's all right, Aunty Jo, it was easy!' Amazingly Paddy's small face had fallen into the stern, adult lines of his father's. She stared down at him, her shining black hair falling around her face and caressing her flushed, smarting cheek.

'Say you're sorry!' Paddy yelled, swinging wildly, pulling his shoulders back so his compact little body looked inches taller.

An ache of tears was pressing at the base of Jo's throat. 'Stop, darling!' she pleaded mildly. 'It doesn't matter!'

'It *does* matter!' Paddy's hot blue gaze didn't fall away from the lake. 'Why did he hit you?'

Jo made an attempt at humour for the child's sake. 'All men do silly things at different times.'

'They don't hit ladies!'

'Not if they're gentlemen!' It was quite easy to laugh, and Jo did, embracing Paddy's stiff frame. 'Come away now. I'm going to ask Uncle Marsh to let us camp out on the very first free evening. Would you like that?'

'In a moment, Aunty Jo,' Paddy said kindly. His small face was still suffused with rage and he was looking at Blair with loathing and disgust.

'For God's sake go away, and take that child with you!' Blair called grimly, standing sodden and uncertain in the lake.

'How wet you are!' Jo said thoughtfully, and there was a wealth of scorn in the words. 'You seem to have a lily bulb on your head. Don't worry, we won't tell anybody about this miserable little episode, will we, Paddy?'

'If we do everyone will be mad. *Particularly* Uncle Marsh!' Paddy announced, glaring. 'He's six feet two, and two thousand pounds. And he's a wild beast when he's angry!'

'But after all there's no danger. I have you, Paddy!' Jo tried to distract him. 'Have you had your breakfast?'

'No. I saw you from upstairs and I ran down to meet you. Ellen said I could. I was going to bite *him*, but instead I pushed him in the lake.'

'Either way you won the battle!' Jo put her arm

around him and turned him about, using a little force. 'Come on, pardner, let's go up to the house.'

They didn't look back but continued to walk slowly up the slope, Paddy holding on to Jo so that she wouldn't stumble, though he tripped a couple of times himself, his quick temper not yet extinguished. The recent scene Jo so much regretted was not going to be dismissed from his mind too easily. Never in his young life had he seen such a thing, and he was going to do his utmost to protect Jo. If he told Uncle Marsh Lord knew what would happen. Even thinking about it made him feel better. Nearing level ground he swung around in front of Jo, forcing her to a halt.

'Bend down,' he said as though he had suddenly thought of an instant cure-all, 'and I'll kiss it better!'

'That would be lovely!'

Towards mid-morning, Julie came down and quite rightly claimed her fiancé. Blair even rose from his chair on the veranda to greet her with some relief. Since Blair didn't ride and he wouldn't know where he was going anyway they all saw Julie take the wheel of the station wagon. She didn't wave, caught up in her coming ordeal, but took off immediately to discuss what was very much her and Blair's affair. Nothing on earth would make her give him up and she was certain he would settle down after the initial shock. Certainly she had very obvious claims on him, and she was far more determined than anyone had ever yet suspected.

Jo sank immediately into Blair's vacated planter's chair and looked down at the children's efforts. Nara, an accomplished and highly imaginative natural artist, had been giving them painting lessons and they were making real progress, especially Jenny, who had inherited her father's gift for draughtsmanship. Nara was drawing a totem pole with a bird's head at the carved apex and all sorts of designs on the barrel. She had considerable native talent and Jo was wondering how she might best turn it to some commercial advantage, though Nara and the twins were quiet happy on Malakai, their chosen place in the sun. Paddy was using lashings of red, white, black and yellow, but Jenny was sketching away seriously, admiring Nara's composition from time to time. When Philippa in riding gear suddenly came around the side of the house and mounted the veranda Nara and the children said hello politely and continued with their drawing, but Philippa gestured imperiously towards Jo.

'If you're looking for Marsh, he's down at Camp Two.'

She looked unusually tense and Jo took it as a sign that something had gone wrong. 'I wasn't, actually!' she said lightly.

'I've an idea he's looking for you. Anyway, now you know where to find him. I have to get away home!' She walked away quickly, and suddenly the blue sky seemed to call Jo. She was thinking she'd love to ride out and meet Marsh. She felt a need to be encompassed by his strength and personality. There was nothing sinister about Marsh, nothing weak, or vicious or obsessed. She stood up and the children, attracted, looked up.

'Would you mind if I rode out to see Uncle Marsh? I won't be gone for more than an hour.'

'Is it urgent?' asked Jenny.

'Well, I'd like to get a few matters cleared up as soon as possible.'

'I won't leave them alone, Miss Jo!' Nara said, smiling. 'Stay alonga time!'

Jo returned the smile warmly. 'It's just an hour.'

'Are you going to tell him you-know-what?' asked Paddy, drawing in a bull ant, then a wallaby.

'We're going to forget that!' said Jo firmly.

'All right!' he shrugged, though he didn't understand.

'I'm going to speak to him about camping out!'

'Oh, beaut!' both children chimed in at once.

It didn't take Jo long to get underway. One of the boys saddled up Honey for her and she headed across the home paddocks in the direction of the mustering yards known as Camp Two. By the time she reached the first watercourse the sun was hot enough to make her shirt stick clammily to her body and she rode gratefully into the occasional shade of a stand of bauhinias, the spent blossoms raining down on her head and collecting in the upturned brim of her wide straw hat. One of these days she would get herself something more suitable, like the elegant stetson Philippa wore. Mindful of snakes, she kept out of the long grass as she entered the scrub, and a wallaby jumped out in front of her and almost succeeded in startling the placid Honey.

They came down on the creek and splashed across it. Jo searched the other side of the bank for sign of the men or any recognisable sounds, then struck off towards the open country, the great grassy flats that ran on for ever. What whim of Philippa's had made her tell Jo where Marsh was to be found?—unless it was a stupid hoax and she was going in the wrong direction. Only a few strides away an emu rose up out of the grass and ran on before them, its unfeathered legs making strides of nine feet and more with ease. It turned about a little vaguely, then doubled back like a jet. It was just what Jo needed. It took her a good five minutes trying to hold Honey, and when the emu finally ran off she clung to Honey's satiny neck in a near-paroxysm of relief.

Away in the distance was a familiar phenomenon, a travelling cloud of dust. She rested back in the saddle, her glittering eyes trying to make out what it was. Slowly the cloud took form, each flying body uncovered, and she sat as if hypnotised, then twisted to look around her, her reaction astonishment. Racing across the plain like wildfire, fast bearing down on her, was a mob of wild horses, a stallion and its harem band and a string of half grown fillies and colts. They had been on the move for nearly an hour and they were being driven towards the silver bow of the river by a team of stockmen.

It was unbelievable—a stampede. And even in her panic Jo found the sight incredibly stirring. The cloud of dust was swirling nearer and now she could hear the drumming, insistent and powerful, vibrating the flats. Honey became excited and started to reef. Where once the landscape had been empty except for a coasting eagle now the flowering flats throbbed to the sound of pounding hooves. Down along the river the birds rose from the trees and curled away into the blue sky in waves of white and rose-pink; corellas and galahs. Honey's muscles were twitching under her gleaming skin and Jo turned her head around and rode. If she was trampled to death she wouldn't be able to blame anyone. If somehow she survived she would be able to blame Philippa—an enemy in the grand fashion.

Horsemen broke out in a long line. They had sighted her, and if they cursed her sudden, threatening appearance, they all broke out in a cold sweat for her.

Jo couldn't turn in the saddle or look back, even if every moment she expected an avalanche of horseflesh to move down on her. Despairingly she felt herself jerked sideways. Why had she so foolishly boasted that she would make a good rider? She hadn't the experience to ride this one out, and Honey, wild-eyed, was heading straight for a dense wall of scrub. Jo jerked on the reins and lowered her head, clinging hard with her legs to the chestnut's flanks.

From out of the whirling darkness on either side of her, men were riding, superb horsemen and trained at heading off cattle or the thirsty, frightened brumby band. Whips cracked and lashed and shouted commands seemed to hurl around the heavens. One rider flowed up beside her, riding hell for leather, jamming his horse up against the quivering, screaming mare, calling to Jo so that she trusted him entirely to do what he asked. Iron hands bit into her ribs, so she felt they must crack, then she was swung out of the saddle and up before Marsh's hard body, every tense muscle braced, while the wind whistled past them and the thundering hooves suddenly wheeled away and broke their mad gallop.

Yells shattered the air, then there was a curious silence as the brumby leader, a tall, thickset bay stallion of tremendous endurance, two lassos around its neck, came to a slobbering halt. Instantly, as though on command, the harem stood quietly, badly scared but empty of direction. Every sweating body, black, bay and the beautiful silvery-grey, was caked in red dust, mares and foals, all of them wild and unused to restraint of any kind, while the stockmen formed a circle around them. Some would be kept for breaking and the others would be turned out with their stallion again.

The dust was only just beginning to clear and a little further along an aboriginal boy had caught Honey, soothing her down, so after a little while she walked back quietly to join the mob. Marsh reined his beautiful palomino mare to a halt, glancing down at Jo's pronounced pallor.

'What else are you going to spring on me?' he asked, not in the least gallantly. 'They say things go in threes!'

'Am I still alive?' Gingerly she touched her aching breastbone.

'Only just. Either you like frightening the living daylights out of me or you're suicidal. Which is it?'

'Believe me, I'm sorry!' She leaned back against his supporting arm. 'I had no idea you were driving the herd in.'

'Yet you knew where we were?'

'Oh, don't talk about it!' she begged jaggedly, thinking of Philippa's lethal intentions. 'I'm a wreck!'

'Stick around and I'm afraid my own nerve might go!' Marsh's black eyes were glittering and he was pale under his deep tan.

'The fright of the century!' she said, turning her dishevelled head along his hard chest. She was very near tears, trembling with relief and her searing love for him. He was holding her very close, almost forcibly, but she didn't want to shift. 'What an ordeal!'

'I don't get it!' he said tensely, 'but I will. If you'd been hurt...'

'You really hurt me when you catapulted me out of the saddle!' Jo croaked appealingly.

'If I hadn't I mightn't have got you back in one piece!' He dismounted and held up his arms for her while Jo slid into them, her protesting muscles making her tremble all over.

'I can't stand!' she said weakly.

'All right, over here!' He led her out of the burning sun and she slid to the ground, her hair tumbling around her face. She was very pale and her eyes were glittery with suppressed tears.

He stood looking down at her for a moment, then he swung away, talking to one of the men in a low, indistinct undertone. A few seconds later he came back with a flask, which he held out to Jo. 'Drink it!' he said curtly, some of the fury of fright still in his face.

'Well, you know...' she protested, but he removed the stopper and put the flask purposefully into her hand.

It didn't seem wise to resist. The fiery liquid burned violently all the way down, but it seemed to stop the worst of her trembling. Bart, the head stockman, had gone for the jeep and he was bringing it up now, negotiating the crossing. Marsh let Jo remain in the same position for a few moments, then he bent over her to help her to her feet.

'Come on, Jo, you can't stay here!'

She moaned and stood up shakily, swaying a little, more in reaction than any passing effect of the brandy. All of the men sat their horses or stood stock still appraising her condition. She had given them all an appalling fright, but the speed of the Boss's reactions were legendary. Jo looked up at them all staring numbly at her and she tried a smile.

'Thank you!'

Bart. the closest to her, swept off his dusty hat. 'How are you feeling, miss?'

'Peculiar!' she smiled.

'That's only natural, miss. I'm in a state of the jitters myself!'

'I'm sorry I caused such trouble!'

Bart screwed up his sun-weathered face. 'We weren't expecting you, like!' he explained.

'I wasn't expecting you either!' Jo returned with faint humour, and Marsh turned to his foreman.

'Spell the men a little longer, then get the horses into the yards. I'll take Miss Adams up to the house.'

Bart nodded, tipped his hat to Jo, then walked away briskly to pass on the order, while Marsh escorted Jo towards the waiting jeep. Only his eyes registered any expression and he made no further comment on what seemed to be reckless and dangerous behaviour. Jo sagged in the seat swamped by the pretty neurotic desire to fall into Marsh's arms and stay there for ever. She made a determined effort not to fall sideways, and fainting wouldn't help anybody. There was a suggestion of menace about Marsh, a tension in his hard, lean body that could flare into anything.

A small plane rose out of the trees, climbing towards the sun. Jo looked up at it with a strange faraway expression in her eyes. 'There goes your girl-friend!'

The road ahead seemed to require concentration, because he didn't shift his gaze. 'I don't know that we're so friendly!'

'I thought you'd decided to get married.'

'I haven't changed my mind.'

Jo looked sad. 'A bit risky, that one!'

'How are you feeling?' He dismissed her advice.

She stretched out her hands, staring at them. 'Not so shaky!' She dropped them into her lap. 'I don't want to go up to the house yet, Marsh. I don't want to upset the children, and I'm not going to tell them.'

He glanced sideways at her, then pulled the jeep off the track and down towards the lagoon. 'I'm waiting for you to tell *me*,' he said brusquely.

'About what?' she asked evasively.

'Are you trying to drive me up the wall?' he asked wearily. 'You could have been killed. Even Honey could have thrown you. You're quite inexperienced!'

'Leave it, Marsh.' She jerked back her head distractedly. 'It's not worth it!'

'On the contrary, I think we should have a little talk about it, then I'll decide what to do. Hell, it's no joking matter!'

'It's been real fun up to date. Please don't let me be the cause of any more trouble!'

His glance sharpened over her pronounced femininity as though it irritated him. Her skin gleamed in the sunlight and she looked very lovely and curiously vulnerable. She could hear his teeth snap. Impatience, concern, swift anger. Surely Philippa couldn't have intended violent tragedy? Jo's feelings caught in her throat and stifled her. Perhaps she intended no more than a few moments of frozen fright. Even that was bad enough, but Marsh was an obsession with Philippa and she had looked very strange when she had come back to the house, deserted, frightened, in a mute rage. Jo could see her now in startling clarity. Something had set Philippa off, and Jo had the odd feeling it had been Marsh.

In the glow of midday, the surface of the water shone gold. Marsh braked the jeep to a stop, then switched off the ignition, his lean, powerful body nearly hunched in the seat. After a minute he swung out and came round to Jo's side, just leaning against the side of the vehicle looking in at her.

'Do you think I'm a mind-reader?' he demanded.

'You haven't done too badly reading mine!'

'Oh well, I fear for you, Josephine, when I'm not around.' His brilliant gaze slid over her. 'Where did I hurt you?' he asked gently.

Desire overtook her right there and then, but she managed to shake her head. 'Don't feel guilty. You saved my life.'

'Now it's mine!' He glanced away across the shining water and back to her face again. 'How are the lovebirds this morning?'

'God knows!' she said, as though she didn't care much.

He focused on her intently, a faint frown between his marked brows. 'You mean you don't care?'

'Should I?' she asked honestly. 'I just wish they'd go away. The children want to camp out and so do I!'

Marsh made a sharp hissing sound, then a smile twisted his mouth. 'Don't tell me he doesn't want you after all?'

Jo tilted her head back and closed her eyes. 'Don't be ridiculous—and don't talk to me about Blair. I'm nauseated enough!'

'Dear heaven!' She could hear the mocking jeer in his voice. 'You are a one, aren't you?'

She sighed, resting immobile, the colour coming back into her face. 'I was brought up a puritan. I was taught, for instance, that it's sinful to covet someone else's husband. Anyway, my hot blood has cooled. I don't even enjoy his company any more. The wedding will have to be fairly urgent, won't it?'

'I'd recommend it!' he said in a crisp, clipped voice. 'Let them do what they think best. Arranging weddings isn't really my department and I think Cyb's given it all away. I can't think why they came out here in the first place. Only you've got over your girlhood crush, so it wasn't very kind.'

'Then why did you let them come?'

'Open your eyes, Jo,' he said a little grimly. 'I don't want to miss anything and they're very transparent. I was testing you. I'm not very kind either!'

'Was it really as bad as that?' she asked softly.

'You can't imagine!' he said dryly.

Her hair spilled around her face and she looked intensely feminine, the flutter of her racing heart visible against the silk of her shirt. A bird swooped overhead, the most beautiful azure kingfisher with a red breast and back. Jo followed its flight, but she couldn't evade Marsh's brilliant probing gaze.

'I love you!' she said urgently, as though she was offering him a priceless treasure.

'My poor demented girl!' He leaned over and stroked her hair away from her face.

'I know you don't care!' There was an emerald blaze in the depths of her eyes. 'Anyway, you're my friend!'

'I'm that! It would be treason to deny it. Are you going to get out of the jeep or am I going to lift you out?'

'It's O.K., I'd be glad to.' Marsh opened the door and she jumped down. 'I must be out of my mind, telling you I love you!'

'It doesn't bother me,' he said dryly. 'All you've got to do is prove it!'

'I will when I feel better!' She moved slowly around the hanging, lemon-flowered vines. The moist red earth was covered thickly in tiny, delicate ferns. She could feel the adrenalin tingling through her body, exhilarating her. How could she tell him in such an unconcerned way that she loved him? Yet he was taking it just as lightly. Maybe with tragedy averted such a short time ago it was difficult to be normal. Just the sweetness of being with him was seducing her.

For several minutes there was total silence, then Marsh leaned over her and the look of possession on his face was so strong her body twisted up involuntarily as though she couldn't stand being parted physically from him. He was holding her gently but irresistibly and watching the way her face came alive.

'I wish there'd never been anyone but you!' she whispered frantically.

'No, it's a good thing. Anyway, nothing of importance happened to you.'

'No!' she said softly, glad it was true. 'You're my one love. My *only* love. I'm going to love you until I die!'

'You'll *have* to!' he said distinctly, and brushed her eyelids with his mouth. 'I'm not letting you go—not now, not ever. It's about time you realised that. I never had any trouble making up *my* mind. I wanted you from the very first minute. Beautiful Miss Adams, brushing me aside!'

'I didn't!' she protested.

'You *did*. I almost admired it. That's when I decided you were going to be mine. You know how to love a man, you'll know how to mother his children. It all comes naturally to you, my beautiful, kind, loving, clever Jo!' He touched her mouth gently, a smile in the depths of his eyes.

She drew a jagged little breath, brought to wild life, feeling the strength and warmth of his body. 'Aren't you going to kiss me better than that?' she asked plaintively.

'How *can* I, when all your ribs are aching?'

'Don't make too much of it!' she implored him. 'I want you to love me properly.'

'I will soon enough!' he said tautly, still holding back. 'You're a miracle. *My* woman, and you'll never escape me!' His eyes were steady, forcing her to listen and heed.

Jo murmured his name gently, passion and tenderness all mixed up together, ruling her. 'I'll never *want* to. This is shelter and happiness and the most impossible, astonishing love. I feel like a child, newborn. To be shaped any way you like!'

Marsh hesitated, but only for a second, then he tipped her head back, claiming her mouth with a hungry intensity, a total pride of possession that went far beyond words and time and even the limits of the vast kingdom of Malakai. The sun through the trees cast a strange golden glow over them, their bodies leaving a single shadow on the ground. For the time they were together the world was a pulsing ring of fire and they were safe at its centre.

We hope you have enjoyed this romance.
Mills & Boon publish Ten Romances
each month, all of which are of the same
high standard.
Don't be disappointed — place a standing
order for Mills & Boon titles without delay.